SUGAR CREEK GANG
The TRAPLINE THIEF

Paul Hutchens

MOODY PRESS
CHICAGO

ISBN: 0-8024-7033-5

1 3 5 7 9 10 8 6 4 2

Printed in the United States of America

PREFACE

Hi—from a member of the Sugar Creek Gang!

It's just that I don't know which one I am. When I was good, I was Little Jim. When I did bad things—well, sometimes I was Bill Collins or even mischievous Poetry.

You see, I am the daughter of Paul Hutchens, and I spent many an hour listening to him read his manuscript as far as he had written it that particular day. I went along to the north woods of Minnesota, to Colorado, and to the various other places he would go to find something different for the Gang to do.

Now the years have passed—more than fifty, actually. My father is in heaven, but the Gang goes on. All thirty-six books are still in print and now are being updated for today's readers with input from my five children, who also span the decades from the '50s to the '70s.

The real Sugar Creek is in Indiana, and my father and his six brothers were the original Gang. But the idea of the books and their ministry were and are the Lord's. It is He who keeps the Gang going.

PAULINE HUTCHENS WILSON

1

It had been almost three months since I had gotten into an honest-to-goodness fight with anybody. In fact, I hadn't had a rough-and-tumble scrap with a boy my size since the middle of the summer, when the gang got into that fierce fistfight on the slope of Strawberry Hill—the one that went down in Sugar Creek history as the famous Battle of Bumblebee Hill, which almost everybody knows about.

That well-known, nose-bashing battle was in the daytime, when I could see everything. That is, I could see until one of my eyes got socked by another red-haired, freckle-faced, fiery-tempered boy's dirty fist. That boy was Little Tom Till, who, with his parents and his big brother, had just moved into the territory.

At the top of Bumblebee Hill is the abandoned cemetery where Old Man Paddler's wife, Sarah, and his two boys are buried and where he himself expects to be buried someday. His tombstone is already up there with his name on it.

The fistfight I'm going to tell you about right now, though, happened at night when it was so foggy I could hardly see anything, anyway. So if I *had* gotten one of my eyes socked shut, it wouldn't have made much difference.

The battle was like being caught up in a whirlwind full of flying fists, with me—Bill Collins, Theodore Collins's only boy—right in the middle of it, getting whammed on the nose and chin and almost everywhere at the same time and getting the living daylights knocked out of me in the foggy moonlight.

It seemed I was being half killed there in our old apple orchard—which is where the fight actually started and also where I was when it ended. In fact, I was lying on my back looking up through the branches of a big Jonathan apple tree and wondering, *What on earth?* I hardly realized that I *was*. I was thankful that I still *was* on this earth, though, because I had been hit about a hundred times so hard it's a wonder I didn't get killed.

Don't think I am anybody's sissy, though, just because I got licked that night. I could have licked my weight in wildcats, I was so mad. But when what seemed like seventeen boys with two fierce fast-flying fists apiece started swarming all over me, what chance did I have to defend myself?

Poetry, the barrel-shaped member of the gang, who was with me at the time, was getting even more stuffings knocked out of him than I was, because he weighed almost half again as much as I did.

Before I was completely licked, I noticed that Poetry was on the ground with half the seventeen boys scrambling all over him. Their mouths were spilling filthy words that were as dirty as a farmer's barnyard on a rainy spring day when the mud is six inches thick and the cows and pigs have been walking around in it.

Generally when I am in an exciting scrap in which I have to use my muscles on some other boy, I feel fine, even when I am getting hurt. But this time—well, how can you feel fine when a boy as big as the giant in the story of Jack and the Beanstalk grabs you from behind and whirls you around as though you were a feather and whams you onto the ground as easily as if you were a cottontail rabbit and then lands *ker-wham-bang* on top of you?

In a minute now, I'll get started telling you about that battle, how I got into it in the first place, and how I got out alive. But before I get that far in this story, I'll have to tell you something else, or you'll think the way my mom does sometimes when she looks at me with her half-worried brown eyes and says in her anxious, mother voice, "Bill Collins, how on earth do you get mixed up in so much trouble?"

Poetry and I wouldn't have had that fight at all if it hadn't been for Little Jim, the littlest member of our gang, putting a certain idea in my head just one day before Halloween. Also, I had been a little bit forgetful that afternoon and had overlooked doing something Dad told me to do—something *very* important.

Anyway, when anybody puts an idea in my mind like the one Little Jim put there, I nearly always have to do something about it. I just have to.

Dad, who is a sort of farmer-philosopher, has said maybe five hundred times in my life, "Sow an idea, and you reap an act; sow an act, and you reap a habit." I don't understand exactly what he means by that, but both Mom and Dad, probably the best parents in the whole Sugar Creek territory, are always trying to plant what they call "good ideas" in my mind, just as we plant potatoes and corn and beans in our garden. They are also always trying to pull other ideas *out* of my mind, the way I have to pull weeds out of our garden or cornfield.

We certainly have a lot of different weeds around our farm—jimsonweeds, for example. Those, when they are grown up, are tall and coarse and rank-smelling. They have pretty trumpet-shaped flowers but are very poisonous. Ragweeds are about the meanest weeds in our neighborhood and are the summertime cause of Dragonfly's hay fever—Dragonfly is the small, spindle-legged, crooked-nosed member of our gang. Then there's burdock, whose flowers turn into burrs and stick to any boy who brushes against them in the fall or late summer. We also have Canadian thistles, which swallow-tailed butterflies like the nectar of, and Queen Anne's lace, which is Dad's most hated weed, even though its heads are like lace and Mom thinks they are pretty. Queen Anne's lace has very stubborn roots. If you leave even one plant for a year, next year there is a whole family of them, and, as Dad says, "The summer after that, a whole fieldful of them." They will even take over your whole farm if you let them.

I think Dad was afraid some crazy ideas would get started in my redheaded mind and take over his whole boy.

There was one boy in our neighborhood whose mind *had* been taken over, and that was Bob Till, who was Little Tom Till's big brother and lived on the other side of Sugar Creek. Their father never went to church and was always swearing and getting into trouble, often getting drunk and having to go to jail for a while. Big Bob's mother was the unhappiest mother in the whole Sugar Creek neighborhood. Bob had jimsonweed and ragweed and Queen Anne's lace and quack grass in about every corner of his mind, and his father had probably planted them there.

Anyway, I was telling you about the idea that Little Jim had accidentally sowed in my mind that sunshiny day before the moonlit fight in the orchard.

I was at the side of our front yard at the time, not far from the iron pitcher pump and between it and the plum tree, digging up Mom's old tulip bulbs and planting brand-new imported Holland bulbs in their place. The next spring we would have what would look like a long, straight rainbow starting about six feet from the pump and stretching in the direction of the plum tree.

One of the prettiest sights there ever was around our farm was Mom's tulip bed, which last year, for some reason, hadn't done so well. Every spring, except last year, there were about fifty of them in a long, pretty row. Mom said that each one reminded her of a small child holding a tiny colored cup toward the sky for the sunshine and the rain to fall into.

As much as I didn't like to work sometimes, I was always glad to do something like what I was doing that nice warm Indian summer day. The sun was pouring out millions of sunbeams all over the place, and all kinds of different-shaped colored leaves from ash and maple and elm and other trees were saying good-bye to their tree parents, which had taken care of them all summer, and were falling down onto the ground where they would wait for winter to come and bury them in a white grave.

It certainly felt good digging up those spade-fuls of nice, brown, still-warm sandy loam, scoop-ing my hands into it, picking up and placing in a little pile all the old, small bulbs that Mom was going to throw away, and then putting in where they *had* been those nice, big, imported Holland bulbs. The new ones would sleep all winter, and then in the spring the sunny weather would pull them up through the soil, and they'd be one of the first flowers for us to enjoy.

That was another reason I was glad to do the work—one of the happiest sounds a boy ever hears is when his tired mother, who is working in the kitchen, all of a sudden looks up with a happy smile on her face and exclaims cheerfully, "Just look at those *beautiful* tulips!

Aren't they gorgeous?" The tulips are right where Mom can see them best through the screen of our back door, and that is what she says nearly a hundred times every spring.

I didn't even know Little Jim was coming over to our house that day until I heard his small voice behind me. Looking up from what I was doing, I saw his mouse-shaped face. He had one of the cutest grins in the whole territory, and for a minute I thought it looked like a possum's grin.

A possum, you know, is the only pouched mammal that lives around Sugar Creek. It is what is called a "marsupial." In fact, I had just learned from a book Dad gave me for my birthday that the possum is the only marsupial that lives in North America and is the only mammal in North America that has a little outside pocket in which it carries its babies. The mother possum carries as many as six or even twelve cute little, blind, helpless, hairless creatures in her pocket for about six weeks after they are born. After that, they climb out and crawl all over her grizzly gray-haired back.

Sometimes a mother possum will arch her tail up over her back, and those cute little possum children will hold onto it by their own strong tails, with their heads down and their front feet clinging to the hair of her back and sides as she goes around looking for food. Their food is most anything, such as birds or their eggs, minnows, frogs, fish, insects, or fruit.

One of the most interesting things about a

possum is that nearly always when you catch one, or when it knows it is about to be caught and is scared half to death, it will pretend to be completely dead. It will curl itself up into the smallest ball it can and lie very quiet with a sickly, simple-looking, sad smile on its pointy-nosed face, as much as to say, "My *body* is dead, but my *mind* is not, and I am very happy about it."

The only thing was, Little Jim's grin wasn't simple, but for a minute, because he has a mouse-shaped face that is also shaped like a possum's, he did make me think of the only North American marsupial there is.

"Hi there, red-haired, freckle-faced Bill Collins, Theodore Collins's only son!" he said mischievously.

"Hi, Little Jim Foote."

"What do you think you are trying to do there, anyway?" he asked me.

"I don't think—I just work. My mother does the thinking for me."

"I work like that, too, sometimes," he answered, and his grin looked even more like a possum's grin than a possum's does.

"What you all dressed up for?" I said, starting to work again.

"Going to church," he said.

"To church? This isn't Sunday."

"Mother's on the committee for the banquet, and Daddy's taking her over to help decorate."

"What banquet?" I asked.

"Don't you know? The father-and-son banquet in the basement of the church. We get a free supper and get to see some movies about Old Man Paddler's missionary work up in Alaska."

"I know it," I said. "I just wanted to see if you did."

I must have had a sad tone in my voice, because he asked, "Aren't you glad? A free supper and everything!"

"But that's Halloween night," I answered, "and we won't get to wear masks or go trick or treating or anything!"

"Aw, who wants to do *that*?" Little Jim said scornfully, "That's little-kid stuff," as if he didn't care to believe that he was the only one of the Sugar Creek Gang who was little enough to be called a little kid. But maybe, like most any boy his age, he thought he was bigger than he was.

It had been two whole years since I had been as little as Little Jim was, which means I had lived through two more whole, wonderful Sugar Creek springs, two more great summers, two more autumns in which there were two sun-shiny October Indian summers, and two more long, cold, snowy winters. That is twenty-four more months—more than seven hundred and thirty days—more than Little Jim had lived. And that made me a whole lot older than he was.

Also, I would *always* be two years older. I hadn't been a little kid for a long time.

So I answered Little Jim, "Yeah, I know, but when you're disguised in old clothes and wear-ing a mask, nobody is going to know who you are, and it's worth pretending to be a little guy for all the candy and peanuts and popcorn and stuff you get!"

Then Little Jim surprised me by saying, "Maybe that's the idea. My mother says that if all the boys of the Sugar Creek Gang are at the banquet, they won't get blamed for any damage any other boys do to people's property."

And maybe Little Jim's mother was right. Nearly every Halloween I could remember, things had happened around Sugar Creek that nobody in his right mind, if he had one, would be guilty of doing. There were such doings as dragging shocks of corn out of cornfields and standing them up in the roads or in people's front yards, taking gates off hinges and letting cows and sheep and pigs run all over everywhere, setting the gates somewhere else, unfastening people's rowboats and letting them float down the creek, letting air out of automobile tires, upsetting small farm buildings . . .

And sometimes some of the things that were damaged cost the farmer or whoever else they were done to a lot of money to get them repaired. So maybe Little Jim's mother had a good idea. If the Sugar Creek Gang was at the banquet, eating a free supper and seeing a missionary movie, our parents and the sheriff and the town marshal wouldn't have to wonder if *we* were to blame for any expensive Halloween pranks.

All of a sudden, Little Jim said, "They're going to take up a special offering for the missionary speaker, and my father says I can give two dollars if I want to."

And that was one of the ideas that got planted in my mind and was part of the cause of the fight in the apple orchard.

Little Jim explained it to me—his dad was one of the members of Old Man Paddler's missionary board and knew ahead of time what they planned to do. The dinner for the fathers and sons was to be free, but after it was over there would be what our church called a "free-will offering" to pay for the dinner, and the money that was left over would be used to pay for preaching the gospel to the Indians and Eskimos and others who lived in Alaska.

"Mother is going to give five music lessons," Little Jim went on.

I knew that meant she would give ten whole dollars, because she received two dollars apiece for the piano lessons she taught. Little Jim got his lessons free, though, and he was one of the best players in the whole county.

"Circus wants to give three muskrats if he can catch them, but he has only caught one so far," he said.

I knew that meant that Circus, the acrobat of our gang, was going to try to give three dollars to the missionary offering at the banquet, since a muskrat fur was worth a dollar a pelt that fall.

Last year, Circus had had a trapline along Sugar Creek and the bayou and had caught thirteen muskrats and three possums. His father, who hunted at night, had caught thirty-seven coons with his big long-eared, long-voiced hounds.

I tossed up another spadeful of dirt and said, "How come he's caught only one muskrat so far? I'll bet there are a dozen in the bayou right above the spring. I saw three yesterday myself."

Little Jim picked up a clod of dirt and threw it toward a blackbird that had just lit by our rosebush and was probably looking for a grub to eat. I had been digging around the rosebush that afternoon, heaping dirt high about its roots to get it ready for winter.

Little Jim acted as if he hadn't heard me, so I said to him again, "How come?"

He answered, "Maybe the muskrats are smarter this year than they were last year. They keep setting off his traps without getting caught."

Just that second a car honked out in front, and it was Little Jim's dad's car. It had stopped beside our mailbox.

"I have to go now," Little Jim said, and away he ran, past the rosebush toward our front gate by the walnut tree, whisking along as light as a feather, and for some reason reminding me not of an awkward, gray-haired possum, as he had a few minutes before, but of a happy little chestnut-colored chipmunk dashing from one stump to another along the bayou.

For quite a while after their car disappeared up the gravel road, I stood looking at the long train of gray dust floating in the air, being carried by the wind across Dragonfly's dad's pasture toward Bumblebee Hill.

I was thinking how much easier it was for Little Jim's folks and for Little Jim himself to give a lot of money to missionary work than it was for some of the rest of the gang members, especially Circus, whose father hadn't been a Christian very long and hadn't been able to save any money. He had been an alcoholic before that, and most of the money he had made had been put into the Sugar Creek Bank by the owner of the Sugar Creek Tavern instead.

Then I got to thinking about Little Tom Till again, whose father was still an alcoholic, and how Little Tom had been invited to go to the banquet with Dad and me. I knew Tom wouldn't have anything to put in the offering basket when it came past his place at the table, and he might feel sad inside and ashamed and wish he hadn't come.

Then all of a sudden a cheerful idea popped into my mind, and it was: get Dad to hire Little Tom to help me with the chores tonight and maybe do some other work tomorrow morning and pay him for it. And Tom would be proud to put part of whatever he earned in the offering and also be glad he was alive.

Thinking that made me feel as happy as a cottontail rabbit hopping along the path that goes through our blackberry patch down in the orchard. And before I knew it, I had finished putting in the last tulip bulb and covered all of them with eight inches of soft brown dirt. It certainly felt good to have strong muscles, and be in good health, and be able to work, and just be alive.

The more I thought about my idea, the better I felt. The only thing was, I didn't realize that my being especially friendly to Tom was going to be one of the things that would get me into trouble and into the middle of that fist-fight in our apple orchard.

2

When I'd finished cleaning the dirt off the spade I had been using and had hung it on the toolshed wall, I was feeling so happy inside that it was like a little whirlwind spiraling in my mind. I felt even better than I sometimes do when it's summer and I am splashing and diving in Sugar Creek with all the other members of the gang—not only Little Jim, the littlest and best member, but Poetry, the barrel-shaped one; Big Jim, with an almost-mustache on his upper lip; Circus, the acrobat; and Dragonfly, the allergic-nosed, spindle-legged member.

I was thinking that Tom Till was really a great little guy. I was remembering also that his hair was as fiery red as mine, his face had even more freckles than mine, his temper was just as quick as mine, and it was *his* dirty fist that had socked me in the eye in that other fight—the one that was called the Battle of Bumblebee Hill.

There were seven boys in that tough town gang that day and only six in our gang, but every one of us had two fists apiece. That made twenty-six fists, making almost as many fists as there were bumblebees.

I guess it was the bumblebees that saved the day for all thirteen of us and kept us from getting thirteen broken noses. Boy oh boy, those yellow-and-black bumblebees had probably been living in that little underground gopher den for a long time. So when one of our twenty-six bare feet accidentally stepped on the entrance, it woke up the whole hairy-bodied army, and they came storming out in every direction. In only a few seconds, the thirteen of us were going in the same number of directions to get away, swatting at them with our straw hats and dodging, running down the hill for the shelter of the elderberry bushes. And just like that, the fight was over, which is how six middle-sized boys licked seven bigger boys—the bumblebees helping us a little.

I wasn't the only one of our gang who thought Tom was a pretty nice guy. Circus himself had taken a special liking to him and was always giving him an ice-cream cone or candy bar. And when the gang was running through the woods and Tom accidentally stubbed his toe and fell down, Circus would stop and help him up and act as if he thought Tom was as special as I think my baby sister, Charlotte Ann, is.

Maybe that was because every time they got a new baby at Circus's house—which was about every year—not one of the babies was a boy but was always a girl. As much as Circus liked every one of his sisters, so far he always had to get over being disappointed when he didn't get a little brother.

There was one other reason he liked Tom so well, and I was the first one of the gang to find out about it. He explained it to me one day when we were down at the farther end of the schoolyard. I had noticed that nearly every noon at school Circus would sneak a sandwich out of his lunch box, when he thought no one was looking, and would slip it to Tom.

"How come you do that?" I asked him.

He said, "Do what?"

"You know—give Tom part of your lunch."

"It's not part of my lunch," he said. "My mother sends an extra sandwich every day just for him."

"How come?" I asked.

Circus looked all around to be sure no one else was close enough to hear him and said, "Because when Dad used to be—I didn't always get enough to eat myself. Now that my dad is a Christian and Tom's isn't—"

Circus's voice broke, and he never did finish his sentence. He didn't have to, though. I understood, and it helped me like Little Tom Till even more. I also liked Circus himself better, and I felt more and more sorry for Tom and his mother and even for Tom's big brother, Bob, and his mean father.

Bob Till had been the leader of that tough gang that had been on the losing side of the Battle of Bumblebee Hill. Tom had been a member of that gang, too, at the time. But since he and Bob had moved into our neighborhood, Tom had been playing around with us. Bob was the only boy in the whole territory that was what could be called a "bad boy" or, as

I overheard Dad tell Mom, "a juvenile delinquent."

As I shut the toolshed door after planting
the tulip bulbs and went to get a drink, I
noticed I was whistling "Yankee Doodle."

But then I stopped whistling for a minute
and stood at the pump, remembering that just
one week ago Dad and Mom had been standing at that very place when he had said that to
her about Bob—his being a "juvenile delinquent."

Dad had just pumped a tin cup of sparkling
water and handed it to her with a sparkle in his
eyes, as though he thought she was wonderful.
And Mom had just taken it from his hand and
was drinking it and looking over the top of the
cup at him with a sparkle in her own eyes, as if
she thought he was a pretty nice person himself.

Then Dad said, "Sometimes—not always—
it's delinquent fathers that make delinquent
sons. In this case, John Till is probably to blame
for his oldest boy being what he is."

At that minute, I happened to be hanging
upside down by my knees from the two-by-four
crossbeam at the top of the grape arbor. I
heard Dad with my upside-down ears and saw
him with my upside-down eyes, so I asked him,
"What's a 'juvenile delinquent'?"

Dad explained that it was a boy or a girl
who, for some reason or other, had a twisted
heart or mind and did things that were against
the law or just weren't right to do.

By the time he had finished saying that, I decided I was thirsty, too, so I said, "Let me see if I can take a drink upside down."

Dad gave me an astonished look, but he turned quick, pumped a cup of water, and started toward me, saying, "Anything to accommodate an only son."

I was surprised that Mom didn't try to stop him, as she sometimes does when he tries to do something she thinks isn't sensible. (Dad doesn't always stop.)

Mom not only didn't try to stop him, but she didn't even try to stop me from trying to drink it. So I decided to try it. It was probably a silly thing to do. If you don't believe it, just try it yourself sometime when *you* are hanging upside down somewhere.

With my cup of water in my upside-down hand, I was trying to put a right-side-up cup of water to my upside-down lips and swallow upside down. I managed to get it to my lips all right and was just starting to try to drink when, for some reason, the water spilled over the rim of the cup. Then, instead of running down my chin, the way it would have if I had been right side up, it ran into the two upside-down nostrils of my upside-down nose and up—*down,* rather—into what I decided afterward was a pretty dumb head. In a second, my nose was full to the top—or to the bottom—and the rest of the spilled water ran into my eyes and onto my forehead and my mussed-up red hair.

I quickly dropped the tin cup and almost

dropped myself. If I had, I would have landed *ker-wham-bang* on my head in the path that leads from the back door to the grape arbor to the toolshed. I might have gotten a concussion or something. But I quickly scrambled into a skin-the-cat movement, bent double, caught hold of the two-by-four, and swung myself up onto the top of it, where I sneezed several times in quick succession.

Mom, deciding for sure it hadn't been a good idea, said, "Such nonsensical things you two do sometimes! It's a wonder you don't make a juvenile delinquent out of that boy— the way you let him do any ridiculous thing he gets into his head."

"Such as drinking water?" Dad asked with a mischievous grin. Then added to Mom, "I don't have to worry about him. He'll never become one as long as he has you for his mother."

In spite of my having tears in my eyes as well as pitcher-pump drinking water, I was able to see Dad and Mom looking at each other again as though they liked each other in spite of me. And a fleeting thought flashed through my mind that it *would* be pretty hard for a boy to be an honest-to-goodness-for-sure juvenile delinquent with such nice people for his parents.

Well, as I said, today I was whistling "Yankee Doodle" when I went to get a drink.

Dad saw me by the pump and said, "Run into the house, will you, Bill, and look in my other pants to see if my keys are there?"

I started to go but had to stop at the

kitchen door to keep Mixy, our black-and-white cat, from going into the house with me or ahead of me or after me. She always tries to do that when I go into the house.

A minute later, I was in the downstairs bedroom closet going through Dad's pockets for his ring of keys. I had to do that almost twice every day, because Dad was always changing his pants and forgetting to take the keys out of one of the four or five pockets that each of his many pairs of pants had, and which is four or five times as many as a marsupial has.

Mom, hearing me rummaging around, called from the front room rocking chair, "You won't find any cookies in the clothes closet!"

Now what on earth made her think I was looking for cookies? I had to tell her what I was looking for, because Dad was making a fatherly noise out in the barnyard for me to hurry up.

Mom also heard him, so she told me to get her own ring of keys from her handbag.

"Which handbag?" I called.

She called back, "The brown one. It's on the dresser upstairs."

It seemed I had no sooner started upstairs than I heard Mom's voice calling, "But be *quiet!* Don't knock the house down! You'll wake up Charlotte Ann!"

I went the other few steps up the stairs as quiet as a mouse, but a second later I yelled back down to her again, "They're not in the brown one!"

"Then come on down and look in the

green butterfly bag! I think I left it on one of the dining room chairs!"

I took a half-worried look out the screened upstairs window under the ivy leaves that Jack Frost had changed from green to red. Dad was standing by the cab of the truck with both hands on his hips and both elbows straight out from his sides, looking toward the house. Knowing what he was thinking from the way he was standing, I yelled to him, "Wait till I look in the green one downstairs in the dining room!"

Dad yelled back, "I haven't got any green pants, and I certainly didn't leave them in the dining room!"

Well, there wasn't any use to try to explain anything to him right then. I finished knocking the house down as I hurried two steps at a time down to the dining room, where I raced through all the different compartments of Mom's green butterfly-shaped handbag. Some of its pockets were fastened shut with zippers and one with a snap. The stuff she had in that handbag!

I found the keys, though, and a little later was out the back door, scooting across the barnyard to where Dad was waiting.

"Here's Mom's keys," I said and handed them to him. "I couldn't find yours."

"Oh, fine," Dad answered. Then he added, "Don't forget I have them. I'll just have time to get there and back."

"Where you going?" I asked him. "Can I go along?"

"I would like to have you—in fact, I need you—but your mother needs you worse," Dad answered.

The way he said it made my heart sink. As much as I had enjoyed planting tulip bulbs, I felt sure that what Mom probably wanted me to do was to help with the dishes or something else that was made for girls to do.

"Where are you going?" I asked Dad again.

"Over to Thompsons'—to get a load of hay."

Then I *did* want to go, because Thompson was the last name of my almost favorite member of the gang—Poetry, the barrel-shaped one, whose actual name is Leslie.

I would rather go to Poetry's house than to any other place in the neighborhood. There are so many interesting things we can do at his house. His folks have a recreation room in their basement, where we can play Ping-Pong or checkers or look over his seashells. Or I watch his snails run a lazy race or his pet tree frog gobble down mealworms. Poetry had the cutest little green-and-brown frog living in a glass jar with an inch of water in it and an upside-down small glass in the container for a stool. The jar had a net cover so that the friendly little fellow couldn't jump out.

Also, Poetry always had more mischievous ideas and plans for adventure than any of the rest of the gang. We could have more fun together just by imagining we were pirates, or policemen, or cowboys, or something else a boy is always imagining himself to be.

"Are you sure Mom needs me? Can't I help her when I get back?" I asked with a hopeful question mark in my voice.

But Dad put a sad period on the end of his answer by saying, "Absolutely not. Poetry may have a little work to do himself, and his parents wouldn't want him to be interrupted."

"I could help him help you load up the hay. Poetry and I could go up into their haymow and throw the hay down for you."

"The hay is already down. It's *baled* hay."

That didn't seem to make sense. Our barn was already full of hay, anyway. A lot of it was baled, and it seemed strange for Dad to be going after a load, so I said, "We don't need any more hay, do we?"

I felt a little bit stubborn in my mind about not getting to go, but when Dad says a thing and is sure he means it, it's the same as trying to push over a barn to get him to change his mind. So I only asked, "What do we need any more hay for?"

"To feed those starving old apple trees out there in the orchard—the ones that didn't bear apples last year. They are getting old and scraggly and need some good high-nitrogen hay."

What on earth? I thought, trying to imagine an apple tree eating hay. It really sounded silly. We fed hay only to horses and cows and pigs and sheep around our farm—actual honest-to-goodness livestock, certainly not to anything that belonged to the vegetable kingdom, which is what trees belong to.

I knew Dad was always reading farm magazines and books and trying to use up-to-date methods and ideas, but I couldn't imagine an apple tree eating hay. It was ridiculous.

Dad started the truck then and gave me several last-minute instructions. "You behave yourself this afternoon and do everything your mother says. I'll be back in time for supper. And the first thing in the morning, you can help me feed the trees. We want to get them mulched down before the fall rains start, so the nitrogen in the hay will soak down to where the roots can feed on it all winter. And then, next year we'll really have apples!"

I guess I must have looked doubtful, so Dad took another minute to explain it to me.

"Farmers in some of the Eastern states have been spreading high-nitrogen hay under their apple trees instead of fertilizer out of a sack, and the nonproductive trees have come to life in a very wonderful way. Those five trees next to the blackberries have been limping along for two or three years, hardly bearing at all."

It sounded silly and sensible at the same time.

But I still wanted to go with him. I hadn't seen Poetry since yesterday—yesterday being the last day of school for this week, because of there being a teachers' convention today and tomorrow. All schools in the county were closed, giving all the tired-out boys and girls a three-day weekend.

"Maybe you can bring Poetry back with

you," I suggested, "and he could help us un-load the hay"—anything to get to be with my good friend for a while.

"I can't do that either," Dad said, racing the motor and getting ready to start. "I'm getting the hay from their other farm—on the other side of the creek."

And that was that. I watched him drive through the gate and down the turnpike to the north road. There he turned and went on to-ward the bridge, leaving a trail of gray dust moving along behind him.

I was still standing by "Theodore Collins" on our mailbox, watching the gray dust boiling along after the truck and remembering I had forgotten to ask Dad if we could hire Little Tom Till to help with the chores. I was feeling sad inside—in spite of not having had to go to school today—when Theodore Collins's wife opened one of the windows of our front room, the one next to the telephone, and called Theodore Collins's son to come in and help her.

Almost right away I started taking slow, sad steps toward the kitchen door to see what she wanted. I hoped it wouldn't be dishes, not knowing I was going to stumble onto another strange adventure that very afternoon before Dad got back—one that would make any red-haired boy's hair stand on end.

3

As I have told you, it was a beautiful autumn day. The sky was one of the prettiest blues I'd ever seen. It looked like a big upside-down blue breakfast bowl with a yellow hole in it and nice warm sunshine coming through the hole and scattering all over everything like water out of a garden sprinkler.

By the time I had reached the board walk that runs from the kitchen door to the pump, Mixy was there, too. Even if I had wanted to stop her, I couldn't have, because the second I opened the door she was under and in. With her big, long, bushy black-and-white tail straight up, she marched ahead of me to the living room, where Mom was.

As I followed Mixy, I hissed, "Hey, *scat!* Keep out!" I knew I wasn't supposed to let her in if I could help it. As I passed the stove and the woodbox, I took a quick look toward the place where the lunch dishes are nearly always standing stacked if nobody has asked me to do them yet. I noticed that they were already done, which made me feel a little better about having to stay at home.

Mom was sitting in our red armless rocker with some pretty blue-and-white calico or gingham cloth spread out on her lap. She had several straight pins in her mouth—and shouldn't have had, because she never lets me hold pins in *my* mouth and doesn't want to set a bad example for Charlotte Ann. She didn't even look up but kept her eyes on her scissors as she cut carefully around the edge of a paper pattern. The cutting sound sounded like our horses in the barn when they are chewing corn or hay. That is one of the most interesting sounds a boy ever hears around a farm, especially if he is in the barn at night and everything else is quiet—a horse eating hay or corn or other horse food.

"Did you call me?" I asked Mom.

She answered from around the pins. "Who else could it have been?"

"If you need me for anything, I'll be down at the barn," I said cheerfully, starting toward the kitchen door.

But I was stopped by Mom's voice saying very firmly, *"Stop!"*

I had already guessed what she wanted me to do before she said, "Get your shoes off. I want you to stand on a chair for me."

Then I *did* wish I was with Dad in the truck. Whenever Mom wanted me to stand on a chair and told me like that, I knew it meant she wanted me to be what she called "a live dress form." She would put some kind of an unfinished girl's or woman's dress over my head and pull it down over my shoulders as if it was an extra-long shirt. And then I would have to stand and stand and stand and stand. And also stand and stand and stand, while the seconds, which seemed like minutes, and the minutes, which seemed like hours, dragged slowly past, and while she measured and tucked and pinned and sewed and measured and talked around the pins in her mouth.

Sure enough, that's what I had to do. It seemed Mom was always making a dress for somebody, for herself or for some neighbor. She was one of the best seamstresses in the whole Sugar Creek territory. Some of the prettiest dresses that ever got worn to the Sugar Creek Church or to the Literary Society, which met in the Sugar Creek School once a month in the winter, were the ones I had worn first myself, standing on a chair in our front room.

"Who you making it for this time?" I asked after I had stood still on the chair for what seemed three or four days.

"For Mrs. Till," Mom replied. "So she can wear it to the banquet. She's going to help serve. Oh dear, there goes the phone."

And Mom left me standing there while she went to answer our party line telephone. I couldn't tell from what she was saying who had called, but I *could* tell it was some woman, because right away they were talking about women's stuff, such as baking and housecleaning.

I kept waiting on the chair.

Then they started to talk about sewing, and I kept on standing, still with an unfinished woman's dress on. I glimpsed myself in the mirror above the mantel and noticed I was wearing a mussed-up forehead as well as a dress.

Mixy was on the floor below me. She was arching her back against everything in the room, including the legs of the chair I was on and the living-room table—and also against Mom's ankles as she sat at the phone talking.

It sounded as if Mom and whoever it was were having more fun than a flock of blackbirds in autumn getting ready to start South for the winter. They were talking about seams and stitches and tucks and gathers and needles and thread and hems and other stuff mothers talk about, which they understand and hardly any boy in the world does, and which Dad says is some kind of foreign language that human beings such as men and boys can't understand.

Then, all of a sudden, I looked past my reflection in the mirror and saw through the window that was behind me a cute little bushy-tailed, frisky, bright-eyed red squirrel digging a hole in our front yard, probably getting ready to bury a walnut. Knowing squirrels, I knew that sometime during the winter, when the squirrel would be hungry, it would dig down through the snow and into the ground and unearth that very same walnut and have it for breakfast or lunch or supper or for a between-meal snack. That is one of the happiest sights I ever see around our neighborhood—old Bushy-Tail with his blunt, rounded head and his large, broad ears and short, thick fur. His tail was almost as long as his body and head. Since he was so active, it would be as hard for *him* to keep still, if his mother wanted him to, as it would be for a boy standing on the edge of a chair with a dress full of pins on him.

In spite of the fact that I was wearing a dress with pins sticking all over it—and didn't dare move or get off the chair to sit down on it or I would become a live pin cushion—when I saw that cute bushy-tailed red squirrel whisking around on our lawn and digging a hole right beside our rosebush to bury a walnut, a little glad feeling came to life somewhere inside of me. I felt as fine as I do on a hot, stuffy summer day when I am tired from having to hoe potatoes or weed onions and all of a sudden a cool, sweet-smelling breeze comes scampering across somebody's field of new-mown hay and fans my cheeks and makes me glad to be alive.

"Hsst!" I exclaimed to Mom. "We have company! Look at that squirrel out there digging under the rosebush!"

But my "Hsst!" blasting into Mom's uncovered ear, while she was trying to hear with her other ear something someone a long way off was saying, must have made her feel what Dad would probably call "impatient."

She quickly waved in my direction to warn me to keep still, not realizing that at that very second I was trying to balance myself on my left foot and at the same time see how far I could reach out in front of me with my right foot, with a dress on. Her arm sort of blindly swinging around accidentally struck my right foot and unbalanced me.

The next thing I knew, I was swaying in several directions. The chair I was standing on lost its balance, too, and in a sixth of a second it was like our house had been struck with a tornado. Theodore Collins's only son and his chair and somebody's unfinished dress full of pins went down onto the living-room floor with a *crashety-wham-bang, rollety-sprawlety, sizzlety-plop-stop!* And at the same time what felt like seventeen pins stuck me in even more than that many different places!

I let out a couple of unearthly screams. Mom let out several of the same kind, her voice probably shooting like a scared arrow into the telephone's mouthpiece and scaring half to death whoever she had been talking to on the other end of the line.

You couldn't expect Charlotte Ann, my baby sister, to sleep through noise like that. Within six seconds—or maybe even less—she decided to help us make noise. Even before I started to get up from the floor, she started to cry in the other room. Now Mom not only couldn't hear the other woman on the telephone but probably couldn't hear herself think.

I couldn't hear myself think, either. My thoughts were as mixed up and noisy as the midway of a county fair with the calliope playing full blast and the merry-go-round going around, and a hundred voices calling from every direction. Besides, I had *pins* in me!

I did manage to hear Mom say just before she hung up, "It will have to be good-bye for now. I'll call you later. I hope nobody was listening in. They would think we were a pack of hyenas over at our house."

Well, I managed to live through the experience, and Mom did, also. I found out that actually there were only three or four pins that had stuck me.

I hadn't any sooner gotten back up on the chair and started to stand still for another week or two than I spied something else in our mirror. This time it was a barrel-shaped boy bicycling up to our mailbox—mischievous Poetry himself, my just-about-favorite gang member.

I could have let loose a yell that would have scared a wildcat out of his chestnut brown skin, I felt so good. *Good old Poetry,* I thought. *He knows just when to come to my rescue. Mom won't have the nerve to make me be a dress form while she makes a dress for Mrs. Till—not with him here.*

Generally, when Poetry gets that close to our house, he stops and whistles one of his favorite whistles, which nearly always is a wood thrush's mating call in the spring. Sometimes, though, he lets loose a blast with a wooden whistle, which he is extragood at doing. Then he waits around by the gate till I can manage to break loose from what I am supposed to be doing—and usually don't want to be—and can make a dash out whatever door I am nearest to get to him as quick as I can, which is never too quick to suit me but sometimes is too quick to suit Mom or Dad or both.

But this time Poetry didn't stop. He parked his bike, then swished through that gate as fast as anything, not even closing it after him, and came waddling across the yard, past the rose-bush and straight for our front door. In a second he was knocking a businesslike knock as if he was in a worried hurry.

"I'll get it," I said to Mom, but she stopped me.

"Don't you dare move," she commanded me. "*I'll* get it."

But before Mom could even start to start toward the door, it burst open, and Poetry breezed in.

In his hand he had a small carrying case about twice as big as Mom's largest handbag. His mischievous eyes had a worried look in them as they swept around the room, taking in everything at a glance, such as the heating stove, which we had put up that week to be ready for winter when it came, the davenport against the wall by the window, the library table on the north side by the other window with our red-bound family Bible on it that was getting worn from Dad and Mom's using it so much—especially to study their Sunday school lessons —the sewing machine in front of Mom, and the telephone.

Finally, Poetry's eyes squinted up at me, standing on the chair with a dress on, and he said in a businesslike, half-anxious, ducklike

voice, "Where is the patient? The accident victim?"

With that, he opened his case, and I recognized it as one he used on our last camping
trip. The second he opened it, I noticed it had
in it only a Red Cross first-aid kit, which he also
opened as he sat down puffing on a straight-
backed chair by the stove. He said again, "The
accident victim. The one that screamed a while
ago—I came to see if I could help save a life."

"You mean you heard me yell?" I gasped.
Why, he lived a quarter of a mile away. Of
course, he might have heard *Mom* scream,
because she had screamed toward the window
in the direction of their house. But I had
screamed in the other direction. "You couldn't
hear that far away," I said.

Then he laughed. "Mother did, over the
telephone. I mean—she told me about the
accident, and I grabbed my bag and bicycled
over as fast as I could!"

Mom came to life then and said, "But I
wasn't talking to your mother on the phone. I
was talking to Big Jim's mother."

Then I saw the doctor's fair face turn crim-
son as he stammered, "But—my mother—that
is, she probably was just going to use the phone
and picked up the receiver first to see if the
line was busy."

Well, it was a good idea, and it goes to show
what a mischievous boy Poetry sometimes is.
Anyway, it had given him an excuse to come
over to our house.

As soon as Mom finished with me, which was almost right away, because I wasn't a very good live dress form with Poetry there, I let him dress my wounds with some Band-Aids. Now that I looked at the pinpricks, I noticed they actually weren't deep enough even to scratch through the outer layer of my skin, which is what the books we use at school call the "epidermis." Poetry called it that as with a grim face he diagnosed my case. He said seriously, "You have a slightly pierced epidermis, caused by a sharp-pointed instrument, probably induced by a fall."

"Such long words!" I said.

Mom always did like Poetry and seemed to know exactly how to make him like her. Right away she asked him if he had had his cherry pie today, and he hadn't. While she was in the kitchen getting a piece of pie apiece for him and me, she called back, "Perhaps the doctor would like to treat my son's mother's eardrums."

"I would," he said. "I'm good at that. I just fixed my own mother's before I left home."

We went on outdoors to digest our pie and also, with Mom's permission, decided to go across the road and through the woods to the creek.

Poetry hadn't any sooner gotten outside than he wasn't a doctor anymore but was a hunter. He pulled from his pocket a black-walnut duck call and blew a quick, sharp blast. It sounded almost exactly like the call ducks make when they are scared or excited.

Then he said, "Let's go down along the bayou to see if we can see any muskrats working on their winter houses," which seemed to be exactly what I wanted to do myself.

I quickly went into the house for my binoculars, and in minutes we were running and walking and leaping over logs and dodging around brush piles as we scrambled along through the nice autumn weather and the falling leaves toward the bayou.

"Let's stop at the spring first," Poetry said behind me.

When I asked him why, he answered, "To see if there are any coon tracks. There are a lot of coons around this year."

Just then I stumbled over a fallen branch and fell sprawling. Poetry, who was still behind me, fell over me, and both of us landed in a tangled-up scramble in a big pile of leaves. Feeling lazy anyway, we decided to stay there and wallow a while, the way hogs do in a mud puddle.

We had been lying in the leaves maybe five minutes when I heard the *crunch-crunch-crunchety-crunch-crunch* of something running through the woods. A second later I heard a boy's noisy sneeze and, looking up, saw a crooked-nosed little guy dressed in a cowboy outfit.

As soon as he saw us, he came whooping it up toward us, yelling like a banshee, waving a toy gun, and shouting, "Where is he? I'll shoot him deader than a doornail!" It was Dragonfly.

He slowed down when he reached the edge of our leaf pile and looked down at me with a surprised expression on his face. "Oh, there you are! Are you all right? I thought you got half killed when you fell off that chair!"

"Who told you?" I asked as I rolled over and sat up.

He grinned and answered down at me, "Mother heard it on the phone."

"But my mother wasn't talking to your mother," I said.

"I know it," he answered. "But she accidentally heard it. I thought maybe somebody was on the warpath so I hurried over to help. Your mother sent me down here to find you."

The three of us went on to the spring. Dragonfly was being careful not to walk in the mud. His outfit was so new and his brown shoes so shiny that he didn't want to get them soiled.

"Where are the coon tracks you were looking for?" I asked Poetry.

He grinned, saying, "I was just thirsty and wanted to be sure you would go to the spring with me."

Pretty soon the three of us had had a drink apiece and, pretending to be Indian scouts, were moving stealthily along the rail fence that skirts the top of the hill just above the bayou. We were keeping ourselves out of sight behind the evergreens that grew along the fence itself, hoping to get a glimpse of muskrats at work, which pretty soon we did.

Right out in the middle and also up and

down the edge of the bayou were some cute three-foot-high brown houses shaped like Eskimo igloos, which the muskrats used for homes.

When it was my turn to use the binoculars, I focused them on a moving V-shaped trail of water out in the middle of the bayou. There a little blunt-headed muskrat, which I knew had webbed hind feet, went swimming along from one igloo-shaped house to another. He was probably using his flat tail for a rudder to help him swim and to steer his body in the direction he wanted to go.

I got to thinking how the One who had created all the wild things around Sugar Creek had made them exactly right for the kind of life they had to live. And it seemed wonderful that He had made so many different kinds of animals for a boy to enjoy watching and to help make him glad to be alive—which I was most of the time.

Pretty soon it would be winter, I thought, and that cute little quadruped would really need his fur coat, especially if he was going to swim around under the ice. The bayou always freezes over in the wintertime. I also was thinking how the little muskrat children could go in swimming anytime they wanted to and could get their clothes all wet and their parents wouldn't care. And they could dive into their houses from outdoors without having to wipe their feet or dry them on a mat. What fun it might be to be a muskrat!

But I was glad I wasn't one, because

hunters, and especially trappers, catch them in the fall and early winter and sell their fur. I was even thinking a kind of silly thought—there was hardly a fur coat worn around Sugar Creek that some friendly little blunt-headed, flat-tailed, web-footed muskrat hadn't worn first, just as I had worn an unfinished woman's dress while standing on a chair in the living room of our house.

I didn't like to think of such a sad thing happening to the cute muskrat I was watching. But when I remembered what a large family Circus's dad had and how hard it was for him to make a living, it seemed all right for him and Circus to make a little extra money that way so that Circus and all six of his many sisters could have nice enough clothes to wear to Sunday school. They all went every Sunday now that Circus's dad had given his heart to God.

It was a lazy autumn day, and for a while I forgot about watching muskrats and just let myself relax in the warm Indian summer sun. It felt good to be resting after my two weeks of hard work helping Mom make a dress for Little Tom Till's mother to wear to the banquet tomorrow night.

That is one of the things I like to do almost better than anything else—lie on a nice bed of long, mashed-down bluegrass and, looking up, watch what is going on in the trees or in the sky. Sometimes I imagine myself to be a bird and I fly all around wherever I want to. Sometimes I am a leaf like the red-and-yellow one that right that minute I saw let go of the twig it had been fastened onto all summer and start on an end-over-end tumble toward the ground, where most of the little leaf friends it had laughed and played with all summer already were. It would have been lonesome staying up there all alone all winter, which once in a while a leaf does—not even letting go when the wind blows hardest of all.

Just thinking that made me wish it was a hot summer day, instead of a warm autumn one, and we could go in swimming once more before Sugar Creek would freeze over and would have a cold, white face all winter. As much as I liked snowballing and skating and coasting and the long winter evenings by the big heating stove at our house, when Mom or Dad and I would play checkers or all three of us crack walnuts or make and eat popcorn or maybe Mom would sit at the organ and play and sing a few songs—and the gang in the day-time would have fun playing in the snow—still, I liked the summers best and hated to think of how soon winter would be really here.

Even though my thoughts were half sad, I liked to think them, and I didn't like to have anybody interrupt them. So I was startled into being half mad when all of a sudden there was a sharp hissing behind me.

It was Dragonfly saying, *"Psst."* That's just what he always says when he sees or hears something unusual before the rest of us do.

Sometimes what Dragonfly sees or hears

first is important, and sometimes it isn't. But this time it was *really* important—more than anything he had hissed about in a long time.

"See," he whispered excitedly, "somebody's coming up the bayou."

I quickly looked and saw a rough-looking man or boy—I couldn't tell which—wearing a coonskin cap and an old brown coat that was the color of the muskrat igloos. I could tell, from remembering the kind of hunting coat Dad wears sometimes, that it would have a blood-proof game pocket in it, especially made for storing away anything the hunter had shot or caught in a trap, so that he wouldn't get the rest of his clothes soiled.

The man or boy was carrying a rifle and was walking stealthily along the other side of the bayou, peering into every place that looked as if it might be cover for quail or rabbits. "Cover," as any hunter or farm boy knows, is a thicket or underbrush or anything else that shelters "game," which around Sugar Creek generally means rabbits or quail or raccoon or possum or fox or muskrat or squirrel or bobcat or wolf or even bear.

The short, chubby man or boy was holding his gun in readiness so that, if he found any animal, he could shoot quick. Then all of a sudden he stopped—not more than six feet from the water's edge—and stooped to study the ground.

From behind me Poetry whispered. "He's looking for muskrat signs, I'll bet you."

I focused my binoculars on him. Right that minute he stood his gun against the trunk of an old willow tree. Then he stooped low at the water's edge, reached out with his right bare hand, and plunged it under the water. Before I could have said "Jack Robinson Crusoe," his hand came back up with a long, slender forked stick in it. And what I saw made me gasp. Dangling on the end of the stick was a chain, and on the chain was—

"*Hey!*" I screamed under my breath to Dragonfly and Poetry. "He's got a muskrat, and it's in Circus's trap!"

"Let *me* look," Dragonfly begged, tugging at my sleeve to get me to give him the binoculars. But I wouldn't, because right that second I was looking at the little brown-furred animal caught in the jaws of the trap. It was a muskrat all right, and it was still alive!

It hurt my heart to see the hunter kill it and shove it into his hunter's coat. But he did. Then he tossed the trap back into the water again.

And right then is when Dragonfly sneezed the way he sneezes sometimes when he doesn't try to control his sneeze. It was like a small torpedo exploding. "*Ker-choo!*" His sneeze was almost loud enough to be heard as far away as the Sugar Creek bridge.

When that "*ker-choo*" exploded into the quiet Indian summer air, it was as if the hunter himself was a rabbit hiding in a brush pile and somebody had shot at him and missed. He quickly looked around in a circle of directions. Then he made a dive for his gun, leaning against the willow. But he stumbled over something and lost his balance. He grabbed for an overhanging branch but missed, and the branch brushed against his coonskin cap and knocked it off onto the marshy ground where it got accidentally stepped on with the hunter's wet boots.

I could imagine how mad *that* must have made him. A second later he scooped up the cap and shook off the water and whatever else was on it. Then he grabbed his gun, and, even before he got his cap on, he disappeared in the thicket of small trees and bushes that border the edge of Dragonfly's dad's cornfield, a narrow strip of bottomland between the bayou and Sugar Creek itself.

4

What do you do when you have been watching what looks like an innocent person hunting rabbits or quail and all of a sudden he quickly stoops, takes a muskrat out of somebody else's trap, and stuffs it into the pocket of his hunter's coat! And then, when your crooked-nosed friend right beside you sneezes, that innocent-looking hunter jumps like a scared rabbit, makes a dive for his gun, stumbles over himself and falls down, makes another dive in the direction of a thicket of bushes and small trees, and disappears!

For a second, the three of us—spindle-legged, noisy-nosed Dragonfly; barrel-shaped, detective-minded Poetry; and redheaded me—stared at each other with startled faces. And almost at the same time, all three of us said our thoughts out loud, which were, "What on earth?"

We argued for maybe five minutes, trying to decide what to do. Not a one of us was brave enough or foolish enough to take out after a man with a gun who was mean enough to steal a muskrat out of a boy's trap.

"Let's just follow him before he gets too far away and see where he goes," Poetry said. He started down along the rail fence. "Come on!" he cried back to us.

And then we heard a noise on our side of the bayou, coming from the direction of the Collins house. It sounded like an animal of some kind, running. When I looked, I saw one of Circus's dad's big hounds, which I recognized as old Blue Jay himself. He was a genuine bluetick—one of the best coonhounds in all the county.

When Blue Jay and Mr. Browne's other dog, old Black and Tan, were on a coon trail at night, it sounded like a half-dozen excited pipe organs galloping through the woods and along the creek.

A moment later we saw Circus himself. "Hey, there, you guys," he called. "That you, Bill?"

"You see me, don't you?"

"Sure," he said, "I see you, but I thought you got hurt. I heard you had an accident."

Then Circus changed the subject by saying, "You guys want to help me follow my trapline? I had to work—didn't get a chance to do it this morning," which I knew was generally the time Circus or his dad went to look at their traps.

"You won't need to look on the *other* side of the bayou," I said.

"Why?" he asked.

Poetry answered, "Somebody has already been there."

In a fast, excited-talking minute, the three of us were telling him what we had seen happen with our own eyes.

Before we were half finished, I saw a fiery

look come into Circus's eyes, a look I hadn't seen there in a long time. It was the same kind of fire I had seen in them once when his father had been drunk and Circus was mad at the people who made and sold and advertised the whiskey and other stuff that make people drunk. I never will forget how he doubled up his fists and with a trembling voice said savagely, "I wish they would just *once* take a picture of my dad when he is drunk and looking like he did tonight and put that in their old papers and magazines! I bet *that* wouldn't make anybody want to buy any!" Circus had looked so fierce for a minute and also so sad that it had scared me, but I was also proud of him for getting mad at something like that.

While we finished telling him what we had seen happen on the other side of the bayou, the muscles of Circus's jaws were tensing and relaxing, tensing and relaxing, and I knew he had his teeth shut tight and was really mad inside.

"Which way did he go?" Circus asked.

"Toward the creek, I think."

"Let's follow his tracks and see who he was," Circus said and started off in a hurry toward the spring and the path that would lead across a small trickling stream and up the other side of the bayou, with us following.

Dragonfly showed that, even with his toy cowboy gun and lariat, he wasn't as brave as he had sounded a half hour before when he came whooping it up toward Poetry and me lying in our leaf pile. "He's g–g–got a gun," he stammered.

I felt sorry for Dragonfly for being so scared, and yet, for some reason, I didn't feel very brave myself. In fact, the very thought of our trailing a man who was mean enough to steal, and who also had a gun, sent cold chills chasing each other up and down my spine.

"We'll just sort of stroll along the other side of the bayou like we didn't know anything," Circus said. "Then we'll study his tracks and follow them. Here, Jay," he called his long-nosed, long-bodied, long-eared hound, "come here." He ordered him to heel—meaning to follow close behind him, which a dog will do if he is well trained. And right away that beautiful bluetick coonhound proved he was.

"How come?" Dragonfly asked.

Circus explained, "Never let a dog follow a trapline with you unless you can keep him from getting close to where you set your traps. Fur-bearing animals are scared of dogs and won't go anywhere near your traps if a dog has been there. They have a keen sense of smell."

With my heart pounding with excitement at what might be just ahead of us, I followed Circus and old Jay on the narrow footpath that skirts the other side of the bayou. Dragonfly and Poetry trailed behind, and every second all of us were getting closer and closer to the place where we had last seen the hunter with the coonskin cap and the igloo-colored coat.

I just *knew* we were going to run into some

exciting adventure, and I was glad Little Jim wasn't with us. He was pretty little to be getting into what probably would be a dangerous experience. I did wish Big Jim were along though, in case we had to fight our way out of something.

In only a very few minutes we reached the overhanging willow, against the trunk of which the man had stood his gun. And boy oh boy! Old Jay, who had been trotting lazily along beside Circus in the path—and acting as if he didn't care whether he was alive, because he was probably thinking there wasn't a coon within a mile of that part of the neighborhood— old Jay all of a sudden began to sniff the air and whine and whimper and to become the most excited dog you ever saw.

When we reached the place where the short, chunky man had been standing when he took the muskrat out of the trap, the coonhound stopped and sniffed and shoved his nose into the man's shoe track and all around it. Then he lifted his head about a foot off the ground and let out a long, mournful bawl like the kind he makes at night when he has struck a red-hot coon trail.

Without stopping to wait for orders from Circus, he started on a long-legged dash into the thicket where we had last seen the man himself.

Boy oh boy! What on earth? I wondered.

When Blue Jay shot up that little incline and into and through the thicket that edged the bayou, it could only mean one thing—he being a coon dog—and that was that there had been a raccoon here and he smelled it. It had set him as wild as the smell of a skilletful of raw fried potatoes would set a hungry farm boy at six o'clock in the evening when he hasn't had anything to eat since noon.

"It's a coon!" Circus cried, and the fire that had been in his eyes, ever since we told him about somebody's stealing a muskrat out of his trap, changed into a coon hunter's excitement.

And away he and the rest of us went—pell-mell, helter-skelter, *lickety-sizzle* into and through the thicket and out across Dragonfly's dad's cornfield, following the excited music old Jay's voice was making. Already the hound was as far as the creek and racing along the bank as fast as his nose could take him.

"Coons don't run around in the daytime," Poetry panted behind us.

Circus said, "Not most of the time but *sometimes*. Hurry up, you guys!"

And we hurried up—running and panting and dodging around chokecherry shrubs and elderberry bushes and marsh rosebushes and driftwood that had been left when the creek overflowed last spring. And all the time my blood was racing in my veins. My half-happy heart was pumping it faster than our old iron pitcher pump can pump water at our house.

For a while the chase was almost like a night chase when Jay and Black and Tan are whooping it up on a hot trail ahead of us. Down the creek we went, past the spring, and up a little incline skirting the edge of the hill.

At the rail fence that runs along the east side of the north road, old Jay's one-hundred-pound body shot up and over as if he was light as a feather. He quickly found the trail on the other side, crossed the gravel road, raced up the ditch, leaped over the other fence, and went on and on and still on.

We were racing after him—falling down, getting up, panting and sweating and yelling to each other in short excited sentences, saying we bet we were trailing one of the biggest coons that ever lived in the county anywhere.

"He's headed for the swamp!" Circus exclaimed.

It looked as if he was right, because by then Blue Jay was so far ahead we couldn't see him anymore.

A little later, though, we heard his long, musical howl change, and he began making an entirely different sound. Circus, who was maybe twenty-five feet ahead of the rest of us, cried back over his shoulder, "He's *treed!* He's got him up a tree! Come on, let's get there quick!"

I was already running so fast I couldn't see straight, which is why right that minute I accidentally ran into a colony of Canada thistles—of which there were about thirteen three-foot-tall, fierce-looking, autumn-browned, many-stemmed stalks. Each stalk had maybe a hundred dry, sharp prickles on it—and a lot of the prickles pierced through my epidermis and into me.

That made me yell even louder than I had when I had fallen off the chair in our living room an hour or two before and some very ordinary straight pins had barely scratched me.

Poetry, who had seen the colony of thistles before I had and had swerved around it, saw me go down. It seemed to remind him of a line of the poem "The Night Before Christmas." He quoted it: "And away they all flew like the down of a thistle"—"they" meaning Santa Claus's reindeer as they went galloping through the sky to somebody else's chimney.

While I was untangling myself and getting to my feet in as fast a careful hurry as I could, I managed to mumble a grumpy answer to Poetry. "You mean, 'Away *Bill Collins* went down—stumbling over a thistle.'"

In a moment, Poetry, Dragonfly, and I were racing on again, trying to catch up with Circus, all of us hurrying toward the place where, away up ahead of us, old Jay's voice was whooping it up under a tree.

In my mind's eye, I was already at the base of some kind of tree and was seeing way up in the crotch of a limb a brownish gray raccoon with black patches of fur on its cheeks and a bushy tail with six or seven dark brown or black rings around it—which is why a raccoon is sometimes called a ringtail.

I had been on many a coon chase at night but never in the daytime. I thought how wonderful it would be to help catch a live coon and how Circus could have its fur to sell to help his dad make a living for his big family of many sisters and one boy.

In another minute now, we would be close enough to see the tree—and also in another minute, another member of the gang joined the chase. This time it was a tall boy with an almost mustache on his upper lip and carrying a rifle. He was the only one of the gang that owned a rifle and whose folks thought he was old enough and big enough to. It was Big Jim himself, our leader.

We had just left the old sycamore tree and were about to hurry on to the swamp to where Blue Jay's voice was booming away, when all of a sudden there was Big Jim with his rifle on his arm and his mustache on his upper lip.

"Hey," he called to us, "wait a minute, and I'll help you."

But Circus was so excited that he didn't stop. He plunged onto the footpath and into the swamp with the rest of us right after him.

In a few jiffies we reached the tree Blue Jay was barking up, and there we all stopped and stared. Instead of there being a gray brown, black-cheeked, ring-tailed coon up there, it was a middle-sized boy—an honest-to-goodness boy!

He was about twenty feet from the ground, standing on a limb and clinging to the tree trunk, sniffing and shaking and looking scared half to death. I saw his face at the same time Dragonfly cried, "Hey! It's Tom Till."

And it was—Little Tom Till himself, and he was wearing a coonskin cap like the one the hunter along the bayou had been wearing. The most surprising thing of all was that at the base of the tree lay a man's hunting coat, and old Jay was excitedly jumping up and down all over it.

What on earth! I thought. *How come and why and for land sakes!*

Then Little Tom Till cried out in a scared voice, "Don't let him h–h–hurt me."

5

It was Poetry who figured out how come a coon dog—who wouldn't normally chase any animal except a raccoon—had trailed a *boy* down the creek and into a swamp and treed him.

"Remember," he said, when he could get his thoughts in edgewise between all of the other excited things the rest of the gang were saying, "remember he dropped his coonskin cap on the wet ground and accidentally stepped on it? Well, he probably got the smell of the coonskin all over his shoes, and old Jay thought he was a coon."

Dragonfly heard Poetry say that and answered, "That's crazy—boys' tracks don't look any more like a coon's tracks than anything."

"Goose," Poetry answered. "Coon dogs don't go by what a track *looks* like but what it *smells* like."

Well, I had been close to the different kinds of fur coats different Sugar Creek women wore, and there wasn't a one that smelled even a little like a wild animal. I even shut my eyes and imagined myself to be standing beside an extralarge muskrat that somebody had sprayed perfume on, and it *still* didn't smell like a muskrat or a possum or even a rabbit—which Dad says is what lots of fancy fur coats are made out of.

But hounds can smell better than boys, so maybe Poetry was right, I thought. Anyway, twenty feet up that tree and right in front of my eyes was a boy in a coonskin cap, and the blue-tick had trailed him at red-hot speed from away up on the other side of the spring clear down to the sycamore tree and past it into the swamp, where we all now were.

One of the saddest feelings came into my heart right that minute, and it wasn't just because Tom Till was crying and scared and begging us not to let the hound hurt him. It was because when I looked at the hunter's coat—which he had probably tossed off in a hurry so he could climb the tree quick to get away from what he had probably thought was a big fierce bloodhound—I realized that the short, stocky hunter we had seen on the other side of the bayou, who had stolen the muskrat out of Circus's trap, had been one of my favorite friends.

He had been going to Sunday school with me, and I had been hoping that before long he would become an honest-to-goodness Christian. I certainly hated to believe he would do such a thing as steal, although I knew his brother, Bob, might and maybe his father too.

It didn't take long to get it into old Blue Jay's long-nosed head that he had been fooled by a boy's wet feet stepping on a boy's ring-tailed coonskin cap and that he hadn't been trailing an honest-to-goodness live coon at all.

We tried to get Little Tom Till to come

down out of the tree, and he wouldn't at first. "I don't want to come down," he sobbed.

Finally he did, though, and I was wondering what Circus would say and do to him and what Tom would say back—especially if Circus asked him about the muskrat he had stolen. It was a sad experience watching that little red-haired guy come down the tree. His blue eyes had rings around them from having rubbed the tears out with his fists—which probably weren't very clean after climbing a tree and also after killing a muskrat with them.

The minute he was down, Tom grabbed up the big hunter's coat, which was a lot too big for him, put it on, picked up his rifle, which I noticed was only an air rifle, and said, "I got to go home. Good-bye, everybody." There were tears in his voice as he started on the run up the path toward the sycamore tree.

"S–s–stop him," Dragonfly stuttered. "He's stolen a m–m–m—" But Dragonfly himself got stopped like a firecracker that only fizzles out instead of exploding.

It was Circus who, standing close beside him, whirled around and clapped a hand over his mouth. And Dragonfly didn't get to finish what he started to say, which I was sure was: "He's stolen a muskrat out of one of Circus's traps."

I got a quick look at Circus's face just then, and his eyes didn't have in them anymore the light that a hunter gets in his when he is chasing a coon. Nor was there any of the angry fire that had been in them when we had first told him about somebody taking the muskrat out of his trap. There was only a very sad and disappointed look in them like a fire that has just gone out.

For several seconds all of us were very quiet, just watching that ring-tailed coonskin cap bobbing on Tom's head while he ran as fast as he could past the sycamore tree and on toward the Sugar Creek bridge.

I knew that about a quarter of a mile on the other side of the bridge was where his folks lived.

Poetry was the first one to speak. "I'll bet he doesn't know that we know for sure he's got a muskrat in the blood-proof pocket of that old hunter's coat."

"It looked like he has about six of them," Dragonfly said. "No wonder he looked like an overstuffed boy when we first saw him on the other side of the bayou."

Well, all the gang members were there now except Little Jim, and it seemed that what had happened was important enough for us to call a meeting to talk it over and decide what to do.

We found out that Big Jim had been up to see Old Man Paddler about the speech he was supposed to make at the banquet tomorrow night, which is why he happened to come along when he did. As quickly as we could, we explained to him what we had seen Little Tom do on the other side of the bayou above the spring.

"What are we going to do about it?" Big Jim asked.

Circus answered, "We aren't going to do anything," and there were tears in his voice. "I like that little guy," he said, "and I just can't believe he would do a thing like that."

"Maybe his father made him," Dragonfly suggested.

Poetry had an idea, too. "Maybe his mother is sick again and they need the money."

Big Jim was sitting on a log with his unloaded rifle leaning against the sycamore tree. He never had his rifle loaded unless he was actually hunting, which is what sportsmen call a "safety measure."

When Big Jim answered Circus, it was with one of the most sober voices I had ever heard him use. His words were, "That doesn't change the verse in the Bible that says, 'You shall not steal.'"

"I know it," Circus answered, "but the Bible also says in another place that we ought to love everybody and—" He stopped and swallowed before he went on. He wasn't looking at a one of us when he finished but, instead, was sort of staring up toward the place in the tree where Tom had been only a little while before. "I think we ought to wait awhile. Maybe we'll find out something we don't know."

"Let's tell the sheriff," Dragonfly suggested.

Circus blurted out a quick loud *"No"* so loudly and so fiercely that not a one of us felt like disagreeing with him.

Dragonfly didn't like to have his idea squelched, though, so he just shrugged his thin shoulders and answered, "It's your muskrat—not mine."

"I'll *give* it to him if he wants it," Circus answered sadly. "I'm just sorry he took it like that."

While we had been talking and having our meeting, old Jay was hurrying excitedly all around the base of the tree he had been barking up. He put his feet on the trunk as far up as he could reach and kept smelling the reddish brown, scaly bark, where I noticed there were a lot of scratches that could very easily have been made by a squirrel or some other climbing animal such as a raccoon. Then he whisked away with his nose to the ground, making wide circles around the tree and coming back again and again.

I had seen him and old Black and Tan do that many a time after they had been on a hot trail and then for some reason had lost it and couldn't find it again. We hadn't had any trouble getting him to understand that Tom Till wasn't any ring-tailed coon, but being a dog and maybe a little bit like a boy who has lost something, he wasn't satisfied.

Then all of a sudden I heard an excited sound away out in the swamp. I was so surprised that I could have jumped out of my skin, because it was Blue Jay's high-pitched voice letting out a long, wailing bawl that was almost ten seconds long. It sounded like what I had always imagined a wolf howl would sound like on a cold, moonlit winter night.

Boy oh boy! The thrill that galloped up and down my spine was like the kind I had had many a time when I had heard that long, mournful bawl or one like it from some other hound.

The second Circus heard it, he sprang to his feet, crying out, "He's hit another coon trail. Come on, let's go!"

Before anybody could have stopped any of us, all of us were galloping after Circus down the path that leads into and through the swamp—the same path we use for a shortcut when we go up into the hills to see Old Man Paddler in his clapboard-roofed cabin.

I guess I'd never heard old Jay act so excited before—not in the daytime, anyway. *It must be a really hot coon trail,* I thought as his high, galloping bawl raced on ahead.

The five of us hurried as fast as we could after him. We were not able to run very fast though—not as fast as if we had been in the woods that go around the bayou. That was because there was so much driftwood and underbrush in the swamp, left there by the creek overflowing its banks, which it did nearly every spring. When old Sugar Creek wakes up in the spring and finds all that melted snow water running down the hills and into his bed, he is like a boy with a bad temper. He gets out of bed quick and starts running all over the place.

On and on and on we raced, through the swamp and out again, with that hound's voice still up ahead of us and traveling toward the hills.

"I'll bet it's a fox," Poetry cried.

But Circus answered back over one of his shoulders, "Old Jay won't trail a fox. He won't trail anything but a coon."

"But what would a coon be doing going toward the hills?" I asked, knowing that coons generally stay close to water when they are being chased.

I had no sooner said that than Blue Jay started running in a wide, terribly fast, nose-to-the-ground half circle. And the next thing I knew, he was heading back toward the creek again.

And there is where he lost the trail for good.

Round and round and up and down the creek he raced, trying to find the trail, but it looked as if he had completely lost it.

After about fifteen minutes of his circling and whimpering, we knew there wasn't any use to keep on. I felt sorry for the dog. He reminded me of Mom going all around our house looking for something she has lost and not finding it—searching in one handbag after another and one dresser drawer after another and in all the closets in the house, still not finding it and worrying out loud about it the way old Jay was doing right that minute. Sometimes Mom would lose something like that, and Dad and I had to stop doing something important and help her find it.

Circus had to have an excuse for his hound, so he said, "The coon probably jumped out into the creek and swam across."

Well, it was getting late, and I was supposed to get home in time to help Dad with the chores. So pretty soon we all gave up, and everybody, including Circus, started for home. At first old Jay didn't want to give up, but Circus made him by promising him, "We'll give you another chance, old pal. We'll come back here some nice damp night and show Old Ringtail a thing or two."

After a little coaxing, Jay came over to Circus and shoved his long and probably tired-out nose into the palm of his hand as if to say, "You're a neat guy not to hold it against me. Besides, it wasn't my fault."

I knew there's not a dog in the world that can smell a coon trail in running water, because the scent washes downstream just like a piece of driftwood.

In about ten minutes we came to within sight of the bridge, and there I heard the sound of a motor. Looking up, I noticed it was Theodore Collins's truck just driving onto the bridge with a load of baled alfalfa hay.

By the time we got to the rail fence and over it, Dad was over the noisy-floored bridge and stopping beside us. And what to my wondering eyes should appear but somebody's boy sitting in the cab with him. *What on earth?* I thought.

The boy was red-haired and freckle-faced

and just my size. He looked almost exactly like me—only maybe he wasn't quite so homely. But it wasn't me. Instead, it was red-haired, freckle-faced Little Tom Till himself with his two big front teeth shining in a friendly grin as he called out the cab window, "Hi, everybody! Want a ride?"

Imagine that! Little Tom Till, who, half scared half to death, had been chased up a tree a half hour ago—and who, as soon as he had come down out of the tree, had scurried away as fast as he could for fear Circus's dad's hound or some of the gang would hurt him—imagine him now sitting in the Collins family's truck as though he was my twin brother and another son of Theodore Collins!

What on earth? I thought again. But it wasn't any time just to think and do nothing. Dad called me to hurry up and get in. We had a lot of things to do yet before night.

I left the rest of the gang to do what they wanted to—or probably what they *had* to do, which was what I had to do myself. I figured maybe one of the things Dad would do first, if we had time, would be to feed our poor starving apple trees.

I certainly felt strange with Tom Till sitting between Dad and me. Tom had a serious face again and was looking straight ahead through the windshield at the gravel road. Dad was driving slowly and carefully so as not to make the load of high-nitrogen hay get overbalanced and tip the truck over and all of us land upside down in the ditch. A load of hay sometimes does that around Sugar Creek when the driver is careless.

"When we get home," Dad said. "I'll have to run into town. The committee at the church needs a few extra supplies, and I promised to drive in for them. You boys want to go along? We'll phone your mother," he explained to Tom, "so she won't wonder why you may have to come home a little later than she planned."

Dad and I had a chance to talk alone for a minute when he and I were in the toolshed getting his handsaw, which had to be taken to town with us to get sharpened. Dad was going to use it to trim some of the apple trees—the fall of the year was the best time of the year to do that. Tom was in the house at the time, drinking a glass of milk and eating a piece of pie, which Mom made him do nearly every time he came to our house. Maybe that was why he came over quite a lot and why I got to like him so well myself.

I explained to Dad what I had on my mind about his hiring Tom to help with the chores and also with the feeding of the apple trees.

"I thought of it first," Dad said. "That's why I brought him home with me."

Dad and I also talked about the main reason that we had invited Tom to go with us to the banquet tomorrow night, which was so that he would have a chance to see a lot of other Christian men and boys and also to hear the gospel.

"Can't we get his father to come, too?" I asked.

"He's been invited, but—well, you know John Till doesn't believe in God, and he hates the church. Wish we could get hold of Bob too, but he won't let anybody love him. He seems to *want* to be a renegade—swearing and stealing and things like that."

When Dad said that about Big Bob Till, I thought of John Till's other son, who that very afternoon had stolen a muskrat out of one of Circus's traps. But for some reason I decided not to tell Dad about it.

Just then I let out a surprised whistle and said, "Well, what do you know? Look what I found!"

Dad, who had been looking at the hand-saw's dull teeth with a question mark in his eyes, looked at what I had just found on the workbench. It was his key ring, which had on it not only the key to the truck and to the car but keys to a lot of other places around the farm.

Right that second I heard the back door of our house open and Mom and Tom's voices as they talked. A second later Tom was out pumping himself a drink from the pump.

That is, I *thought* he was. Instead, he filled the cup and started back to the house with it, saying to Mom, "Would you care for a drink, Mrs. Collins?"

Something about the very polite voice Tom used when he talked to my mother, whom I liked better than any other person in the world her age, made me feel fine in my heart toward him. And it seemed as if he hadn't even stolen the muskrat at all. He had such an innocent expression on his face that it was just as though somebody had taken an eraser at the Sugar Creek School and rubbed out a lot of ugly pictures somebody had drawn on the blackboard.

Mom thanked Tom politely, looked at him as though she thought he was a very nice boy, and accepted the tin cup from his small, still dirty hand.

While Mom was drinking, Dad got a mischievous tone in his voice and said to Tom, "You ought to see Bill drink out of that cup upside down. Want to show him how you do it, Bill?"

"Sure," I said. I reached up and caught hold of the two-by-four of the grape arbor, swinging my feet up and pushing them between my arms and up and over. A second later I was hanging upside down, waiting to give Little Tom Till an education in acrobatics.

But Mom stopped what probably would have turned out to be another sneezing spell for me by stopping Tom from giving me the water.

As soon as I was on my feet again, Dad ordered, "You run on out to the truck, Bill, and get your mother's keys. I think I left them in the switch."

I managed to get a mischievous thought then, and it was, "Did you change your clothes out there?"

He answered in his firm voice, "You go jump in the first lake you come to. I'll be back out in a few minutes. I want to get Mother's grocery list." And he turned and followed her into the house.

6

Right away I thought of something I wanted to do, and I started on a boy-sized gallop out past the pump and across the barnyard, scattering chickens in every direction and yelling back to Tom, "Come on. I want to show you something."

"Coming," he answered in a very cheerful voice.

Even as I ran, I couldn't understand how he could act so cheerful after having done what he had done when he was down along the bayou. Whenever *I* do anything I shouldn't, I always feel sad inside. Also, I thought, how could he be so happy when he had just been scared half to death by a big one-hundred-pound bluetick coonhound trailing him like a bloodhound on the trail of a criminal?

Right away, Tom and I were inside the barn, hurrying across the alfalfa-strewn board floor, and up the wooden ladder to the haymow. There I showed Tom what I wanted him to see, which was a small basketball court Dad and I had fixed up there so I could practice shooting baskets.

Tom made a dive for the ball. He liked to play basketball more than any other game. Our new schoolteacher had started us playing that fall, and Tom was turning out to be one of the best forwards on the team.

But I could see he was only pretending to be cheerful. He was missing nearly all his shots and didn't seem to be interested. He kept looking around at different things and up at the rafters and at some wooden boxes I had put way up on a high log near the roof.

"How many pigeons you got?" he asked.

I remembered then that he used to have ten or twelve in a special pigeon pen on the north side of their barn. "How many you got?" I asked.

He didn't say anything for a minute but quickly shot another basket. Then he mumbled, "I haven't *any*."

"How come?" I asked, just as he stumbled over my foot and landed on the floor.

He was up again in a flash, took a quick squint at the basket, shot and missed, made an awkward scramble for the ball, and fell down again. It was only quite a while afterward that I realized he hadn't answered my question.

Just then Dad honked the horn up by the walnut tree, which meant for us to hurry down because he was ready to go. That is, that's what I *thought* it meant. But when we came sailing out the barn door a little later and dashed across the barnyard toward him, he said, "Mrs. Collins has just announced a change of plans. She's going along with us—but *after* supper. There's too much work to do at the church to get ready for tomorrow, and the Collins family is going to pitch in and help, she says. So get going, boys, on the chores. She'll have early supper ready in two jerks of a lamb's tail."

Tom looked bothered as he stopped by the pump and worked the handle up and down a few times. "I don't know if I can. I promised to be *home* for supper."

But Dad had already settled that with Little Tom's mother. "We just telephoned her," he said, "and promised to get you home by eight-thirty. It'll probably take us about that long to get to town and back and wind things up at the church. You boys can run a lot of errands there, too."

Tom was still bothered, as I could tell when he said, while still working the pump handle, "Who'll do *our* chores?"

"Bob's home," Dad said.

Well, that little guy jumped as if he had been shot at and missed. Then he looked all around quickly as though he was expecting to see his brother somewhere about the house or yard. I could see that for some reason he seemed to be afraid of something.

We got the chores done and supper over as fast as we could, but the autumn days were a lot shorter than summer days were, so it was dark by the time we let Mom and Charlotte Ann off at the church and Dad and Tom and I went on to town to get the extra things the workers at the church would need. When we came driving onto Main Street, I didn't have any idea that I was going to run into one of the most exciting experiences of my life before we left town.

One of the first places to which Dad drove when we got to town was the produce house, where he was going to sell a gross of eggs. The money from all twelve dozen was to be Mom's offering, which Dad himself would give for her at the banquet.

The man at the produce house, whose name was Tim Black, bought not only eggs but chickens and ducks and turkeys and even pigeons. I had sold quite a few pigeons there myself when too many had come to live in our barn and, as Dad said, they had been spoiling the hay. Mr. Black also bought all kinds of furs, such as muskrat and coon and skunk, so I had been there with Circus quite a few times.

Just as we were about to pull up to a parking place out in front, somebody in everyday clothes came hurrying out, made a dash toward a battered-looking automobile that was parked down the street, jerked open the door on the driver's side, plopped himself inside, slammed the door, and started the car. His motor came to life with a noisy roar, and away the oldish-model car went, so fast that I knew if there had been a highway patrolman around, he would have chased after him with his siren shrieking.

I looked quick at Little Tom's face to see if he had seen what I had seen. That dangerous driver was his own big brother, Bob, and there were half a dozen other rough-looking boys in the car.

The expression on Tom's face was even worse than the one he had been wearing when he was in the linden tree in the swamp and old Jay had been whooping it up down below. His blue eyes were glued to the crazy-running car, which right that second came to a corner, slowed down with its brakes screeching, turned right on two wheels, and went on.

Dad, who generally drove carefully, slammed on our own brakes so hard that we came to a quicker four-wheel-brakes stop than we usually do. He said in a disgusted voice, "The idiotic fool! No wonder our highways are slaughter-houses. He ought to be reported. Either one of you boys get his number?"

I hadn't thought of it, so I said, "No."

Tom, who maybe didn't want to say what he was thinking, didn't answer a thing.

We all three went inside the produce house —Tom opening the door for Dad, who was carrying the crate of eggs.

"Well, well, look who's here," Mr. Black, a round-faced, round-stomached, fast-talking, friendly man, said to us as he shuffled around the counter to show Dad where to put the eggs. "These both your boys, Theo?" he asked, calling Dad by the name lots of people around Sugar Creek call him.

"Both of them," Dad said cheerfully and also as if he wished it were so.

I saw Tom Till swallow hard as he looked

around at different things in the produce house, such as egg crates and sacks of feed and empty boxes of different kinds.

I also noticed the worried expression on his face, when, a little later, Mr. Black looked at him and asked, "You boys catching any more muskrats? They're a dollar apiece today."

There were a lot of different sounds in that produce house: chickens cackling and squawking, now and then a hen singing or a rooster crowing, doors opening and closing in some of the back rooms. Also, somebody had a radio on back there. It was tuned to a gospel program, and a male quartet was singing a song we sometimes used in church on Sunday: "Throw Out the Life Line."

The minute Mr. Black said, "You boys catching any more muskrats?" I thought of Circus's *trap*line and in my mind's eye saw somebody in a coonskin cap steal a muskrat and shove it into the blood-proof pocket of his hunter's coat.

I could hardly hear Little Tom's voice as he answered Mr. Black's question about whether he had been catching any *more* muskrats, meaning, of course, that Tom had been catching *some*. What he did say wasn't much of an answer. In fact, it wasn't even a word but was only a kind of worried grunt that sounded like "Huh-uh," as he jerked his head *no*. He started looking around again at the different things in the big room where we were. Then, all of a sudden, he got a frightened look on his face and made a dive along the counter to a high stack of crates near the wall.

At almost the same second, the front door opened. In shuffled a big hook-nosed man with a two- or three-day-old beard on his face. It was Little Tom Till's father—old John Till himself. He was carrying a gunnysack half full of something that seemed to be alive.

When I saw him, another *What on earth?* exploded in my mind. He was lurching crazily, as if he had just come from the Sugar Creek Tavern. He staggered up to the counter where Mr. Black was, hoisted the gunnysack up onto it, and said, "Pigeons."

Pigeons!

That one word went off in my head like a Fourth of July firecracker, and the fastest story I ever thought of raced through my mind like lightning. In my mind's eye I was back up in our haymow with Little Tom Till. He was shooting baskets and acting sad and also looking all around to see if he could see any pigeons. Maybe he was also looking to see if any of *his* were there after they had gotten out of his pen, because pigeons around the Sugar Creek farms went from one farmer's barn to another.

Then it seemed I was seeing old hook-nosed John Till himself going to Tom's pigeon pen when Tom wasn't there and catching some of his pigeons and putting them into a sack and bringing them to town to sell. No wonder Tom didn't have any, and no wonder he had acted as if he didn't want to talk about it!

But that was only imagination. Right that minute in front of my eyes an actual honest-to-goodness story began to happen so fast I couldn't think or see straight. Little Tom shot out of his hiding place behind the high stack of boxes like a red-haired arrow and flew straight for the counter where the gunnysack was.

That brought his father to life. He whirled around awkwardly and lunged at Tom, who already had his hands on the sack. But Tom ducked, and he missed him. Tom darted with the sack behind the first high stack of boxes with his angry dad right after him.

John Till was saying with a fierce, mad voice, "You little good-for-nothing runt!"

But the floor had sawdust on it, and old John's feet slipped. Reaching out to keep himself from falling, he staggered against the boxes and—I saw what was going to happen before it happened, but I couldn't do a thing to stop it.

That high stack of crates and boxes and stuff started to tip over. It was just like a tall tower of blocks falling onto our living-room floor when Charlotte Ann has socked it with one of her chubby little fists. Those fifteen or more boxes and crates came down with a terrific crash.

The same second, almost, the door to the street opened and closed, and through the glass panel I saw Little Tom with the gunnysack in his hand, just before he darted around behind our car and disappeared.

What on earth? I thought. Only it wasn't anything on *earth* but, instead, was a lot of crates and boxes on *John Till*. Right that minute he was lying on the floor, wriggling and twisting. His arms and legs were working like the feet of a big snapping turtle a boy has turned on its back and it can't get over on its stomach again.

Such grunting and swearing I had never heard before as John kept on kicking and struggling to get himself out from under what was on him. I was glad Little Jim wasn't there, because anybody swearing gives him a hurt heart and also sometimes makes him angry enough to fight.

By the time John got to his feet, with Dad and Mr. Black and me helping by getting the boxes off him, his boy was really gone.

"Where's that good-for-nothing son of mine?" he shouted, swearing at the same time.

Well, that fired up Dad's temper—he being my father and having the same kind of temper I had. He said with a thundery voice, shaking old John by the collar at the same time, "*You're* the one that's good-for-nothing, John Till!"

But for some reason John Till seemed not to hear what Dad said. Instead, he swayed as though he was going to fall, and he lifted his right hand to his head as if he had a bad headache or had been hurt when he fell and couldn't think straight.

Then it seemed he forgot why he had come in the first place. Seeing the door, he staggered toward it, mumbling to himself. He yanked it open, lurched through, and started on a crazy man's walk down the dark street.

7

And now where was John Till going, and where had his red-haired boy with a gunnysack half full of live pigeons already gone?

Thinking what he might do to Tom if he caught him, I said, "Excuse me," to Dad and hurried out the door after John Till.

As soon as I got outside, I noticed he was about a half block away, pushing along toward the bright lights of Main Street. So I decided first to see if maybe Tom was hiding with his pigeons in the alley beside the produce house.

"Hey, Tom," I called in a voice that was like a smothered whisper. "Where are you?"

There wasn't any answer at first. Then I heard the window of our car roll down and Tom whisper back, "In here—in the car."

And sure enough, he was—in the back with the gunnysack of pigeons on the floor beside him.

Just then Dad came out, and after he had talked quietly to Tom in one of the kindest voices I had ever heard him use, he said, "Don't you feel too bad, Tom. A man does things when he is drunk that he wouldn't think of doing if he were sober."

Tom sobbed out an answer that proved that, even though his father didn't believe in

God, he himself did. "God will have to punish him for being so mean," he said. "I don't want that to happen." Then he really started to cry.

But Dad kept on using a very kind voice, saying, "God would rather change a man's heart than to punish him. He generally lets people's sins do the punishing in this life, and He only does that when He has to—when they won't let Him save them. Almost everybody in the church is praying for your father. And one of these days he will be different."

Tom Till, not having any handkerchief, rubbed the tears out of his eyes with his fists while Dad put a big hand on his thin shoulder, the way he does to me when he likes me. He said, "You have a very good mother. You know that, don't you?"

Tom nodded his head up and down, still sniffling. "She's better than anyone in the whole world." Hearing him say that made me like him even better than ever.

Then it seemed Tom had all of a sudden decided something. He slid forward on the car seat, opened the door, and slipped out with his sack of pigeons. He hurried with them toward the produce house.

I started to follow him, but Dad stopped me, saying, "Let him go alone. He'll feel better."

I watched Tom through the glass door as, just like his father, he hoisted the gunnysack up onto the counter.

Mr. Black opened the bag and took a peek

inside. Then, to my surprise, he upended the sack as if he was going to shake out whatever was in it. I thought *that* was a crazy idea, because then the pigeons would fly out and all over the place.

Then I did get the surprise of my life, because out tumbled not a half-dozen live pigeons but four dead muskrats! They were not even skinned, as fur-bearing animals are supposed to be when you take them to a buyer, but they had their bodies still inside of them, which made it look as if they had just been caught that afternoon.

Not pigeons, but muskrats! No wonder Tom hadn't wanted his father to sell what was in that sack! No wonder he had made a dive for it and grabbed it and darted outside!

Then something else started to happen. Somebody came hurrying down the street from the direction old John Till had gone. It was a tall man wearing a hunter's coat. He didn't stagger a bit but walked fast and straight, as though he was in a businesslike hurry. At the produce house door, he stopped, turned the knob, shoved it open, and went inside.

Before I could even start to wonder how John Till could have gotten over being drunk so quickly, Dad let out a surprised whistle and exclaimed, "Why, there's Dan Browne! What's he doing in *town?* He told me this afternoon it'd be a perfect night for hunting, and he was going to start as soon as it was dark. He wanted to give two coons tomorrow night."

I always like to run *lickety-sizzle* and throw myself into the center of a whirlwind when it spirals out across our barnyard. And when Circus's dad went whizzing through that open door into the center of what could be a lot of trouble for Tom Till, I was out of our car like a shot and across the sidewalk and inside the room where, only a few minutes before, Little Tom's father had been lying under a pile of boxes and crates. I was carrying a whirlwind in my mind as I went.

When Dan Browne saw those four brown muskrats on the counter, he stopped stock-still and stood and stared as if he couldn't believe his eyes. Then he looked at Tom and asked surprisedly, "Why hello, Tom. You been catching some muskrats?"

The feeling in my mind was almost terrible as I realized that Little Tom Till himself was caught in a trap and wouldn't be able to get away. What kind of answer could he give? I myself, with my own eyes, had *seen* him take one of those muskrats out of Dan Browne's boy's trap that very afternoon. Would he tell the truth, or would he try to lie out of it? I found out a second later when Tom looked all around and stammered, "I–ah–yes–er–no–no sir! I mean—"

His sentence got interrupted then by the ringing of the cash register bell as Mr. Black pushed down on several keys and a drawer flew open. He said to Tom, "That's four dollars." He counted out four one-dollar bills onto the counter.

Tom gulped as his blue eyes stared at the money.

Poor little guy! I thought. *He's really caught in a trap.* And it seemed I could hear two voices talking in my mind. One of them was Big Jim's and the other Circus's. Big Jim's voice was saying, "You shall not steal!" and Circus's was answering, "The Bible also tells us to love everybody."

But in the produce house, Circus's dad's big friendly voice surprised me by saying, "Congratulations, Tom. I hope you catch a lot more. My boy and I haven't been doing so well this year, but maybe we'll catch a few coon tonight. Weather will be perfect if it doesn't get too foggy." He was talking to Mr. Black when he finished. "The humidity and the temperature are just right."

Tom was still looking at the four dollar bills as if he couldn't decide what to do about them. Then he absolutely astonished me by saying politely to Mr. Black, "Thank you very much." He picked up the money, folded it, and looked all around as though he thought somebody might be watching. Seeing me, he let out a great big heavy sigh and said, "Let's go," and started toward the door.

I got to the door first, opened it for him, and we went outside together.

Through the glass panel of the produce house door I could see Circus's dad talking to Mr. Black about something. And even though I was sure I knew what it was, I wished I could have heard it.

As Dad turned the car around and headed for Main Street, I was all mixed up in my mind. I wanted to believe Tom was an honest boy, yet the muskrat I had seen him take with my own eyes that afternoon and the four dollar bills he had in his pocket right that minute proved he was a thief. Didn't it? I was glad, though, that Tom's drinking father didn't get the money, because, if he had, the owner of the Sugar Creek Tavern would have had most of it before midnight.

Sad as I felt inside, Little Tom Till must have felt worse. He not only had the four dollars for the stolen muskrats in his pocket, but he had to leave town knowing his father was drunk and maybe would have to spend part of the night in jail.

Dad drove down Main Street toward LaRue's Grocery, where he was going to stop to get some things for Mom and also for the committee that was working at the church. The only place we could find to park was right in front of the tavern, and that is where Tom and I were ten minutes later when Circus's dad come hurrying down the street in his hunter's coat just as he had before at the produce house. At the tavern he stopped, pushed the door open partway, and looked in.

Looking through the car windshield at the same time, I saw what he probably saw: blue gray smoke as thick as a fog in the Sugar Creek swamp, a lot of noisy men standing at the long bar, and a few women.

Something inside of me made my blood boil. I remembered that Dan Browne used to spend a lot of time in there himself but didn't anymore since God had pulled the jimson-weeds out of his heart.

Then, like a flash, Mr. Browne opened the door all the way and went in.

What on earth!

The door went shut, and I couldn't see in any longer. But I didn't need to even start to worry. A minute later the door opened again, and two men came out—one of them Circus's dad and the other Tom Till's dad, who acted as if he didn't want to come. At the same time, Tom, beside me, dropped down onto the floor of the car so that he wouldn't be seen. I could see that his father was very drunk and wouldn't have been able to see Tom anyway.

And probably he was too drunk to understand what I heard Circus's dad say: "I know what I am talking about, John. I have been through it. It is a life of terrible slavery, but the Lord can set you free. He saved me one night last summer, and I haven't touched a drop of alcohol since—haven't even wanted any."

Old John tried to break away. He stumbled over his own feet and would have fallen if Dan Browne hadn't held him up.

"Jesus Christ is more powerful than liquor, John, if only you will give Him a chance."

But the gospel Mr. Browne was pouring into John Till's ears was like rain on a duck's back—the duck never gets wet. John shrugged himself loose and staggered back toward the tavern door and a second later was inside again.

Pretty soon Dad came back with Mom's groceries, and away the three of us went, out of town and following the foggy country road to the church. Without knowing it, I was also on the way toward a fistfight in which I was going to get the living daylights knocked out of me.

8

We hadn't any sooner reached the church-yard than, by looking at the different cars parked there, I discovered that Poetry's and Little Jim's parents were there, too, and a lot of other grown-ups.

Everybody was working to get the basement ready for tomorrow night. They were doing such things as setting up long tables, putting strips of white paper on them instead of table-cloths, hanging different-colored crepe paper at the windows, and placing a few evergreens over the door and other places.

I noticed they had moved the piano to the north end, where it could be seen and heard best, and I remembered that Little Jim was going to play a solo and Circus was going to sing. They were the best musicians in the Sugar Creek Gang, and Poetry and I were the worst. Poetry sang in a voice that was half like a boy's and half like a man's—and sometimes like a duck with a bad cold.

In the kitchen there were about a hundred new plates and that many cups and saucers. The church board had bought a whole new set of dishes with that many in it. They had to be washed and dried before they could be used—although, when I looked at them, they certainly looked nice and clean. I suppose, though, that all the Sugar Creek mothers were like the one that lived at our house, who always wanted to wash everything every so often whether it looked as if it needed it or not.

I hadn't been there more than three minutes before I noticed that the Sugar Creek mothers were seeing to it that the Sugar Creek fathers were doing quite a lot of the work, which at home they hardly knew how to do at all. Right away, also, they began to see to it that four of the Sugar Creek Gang members helped a little, which Poetry and I actually did for a while.

Pretty soon, though, it seemed the two of us weren't enjoying the work as much as we were supposed to. And a little later, a poem Poetry had been learning, which was funny and also which he was supposed to quote tomorrow night, spoiled everything, and we had to quit helping. He quoted it to me secretly, when nobody was able to hear except me, and this is what part of it was:

A husband who despises housework,
Yet sometimes has to help his spouse work,
Can sometimes gain a quick acquittal
By getting in the way a little.

After I'd heard the poem, for some reason it seemed that there were two too many people in the basement.

Almost right away, Mom stopped me from

awkwardly stumbling around and whispered, "Why don't you boys go outside for a breath of fresh air?"

Almost before she had finished saying it, Poetry's mother said the same thing to him in different words. And because it seemed a good idea, pretty soon the two of us were outside getting all the fresh air we wanted.

Little Jim was inside at the piano, practicing something, and Tom Till was watching and listening to him. Maybe they didn't need fresh air as badly as Poetry and I did, and somehow they weren't in the way, anyway.

I noticed that it was a little foggier than it had been when we came. Almost as soon as Poetry and I had taken a half-dozen breaths of the nice, damp, foggy air, we decided we were thirsty. So we went across the road to the consolidated school to get a drink of water at the iron pump there. It was the same kind of pump we had at our own school two miles farther out in the country.

Of course, we could have used the pump at the side door of the church, but the water in the schoolhouse pump might be better, we thought, since it was farther away from where the work was.

"Hey!" Poetry exclaimed when we got there and he was shining his flashlight onto the pump. "Somebody's taken the *handle* off!"

And that's what somebody had done.

"Maybe it broke, and they had to take it off to get it fixed," I suggested.

We were still thirsty. We decided to go back to the church pump. We were halfway there when a pair of headlights swung into the church driveway. Then a noisy car came to a stop beside the big locust tree near the church steps, which is where we were at the time, and it was Dan Browne. He wanted to see Dad about something.

I went into the overcrowded basement to get Dad, and when I came back I had a chance to hear what he and Mr. Browne talked about. It was about Little Tom Till's father.

"We won't give up on him," Circus's father said. "I prayed for him all week, hoping to get him to come tomorrow night. I thought maybe if I could take him hunting with me tonight and let him see what a difference being a Christian had made in me, I could win his confidence. But somebody got to him with a drink first, and you know what that means. You know what it used to mean to me before the Lord turned me inside out and made me a new man."

Mr. Browne sighed and then went on. "I'm afraid he'll have to suffer awhile before he wakes up. 'Whatever a man sows, this he will also reap.'"

"Poor Mrs. Till," Dad said.

For a few seconds after that, nobody said anything. Then Dan Browne changed his tone of voice and asked, "How soon'll you be through here? It's a perfect night for coon."

Dad answered with a sigh. That meant he was probably wishing he could be in the way a little too much, since he liked to go coon hunting almost as much as he liked to hold Charlotte Ann on his lap and coo over her. But he knew he'd have to stay until the mothers were through, so he said, "I'm afraid it'll be another hour—a half hour, anyway. Where are you going to hunt first? Maybe I could meet you somewhere—say at Seneth Paddler's cabin, if you're going *down* the creek."

They decided that was a good idea.

That gave me a still better idea, and it was that Poetry and I could both go *right now*. If we stayed here and tried to help with the work, we would be in the way, anyhow. Just talking about coon hunting reminded me of the afternoon's chase, and my blood was still tingling with excitement over it. It seemed a shame that the bluetick had had to give up on the coon whose trail his nose had lost in the swamp.

Poetry's father didn't like the idea very well at first, and both our mothers didn't. But when Mom found out that Dad himself thought it was all right—and that we would all meet at Old Man Paddler's a little later—she let me go. She told me I would have to stop at our house first, though, to change into some old clothes, which I was glad to promise to do, being willing to do almost anything to get to go. Poetry already had on his overalls and old shoes and his second-best jacket, which his mother said he could wear if he would be careful with it.

Boy oh boy! To go galloping through the night behind the best pair of coonhounds that ever lived! It was a wonderful feeling that got half squelched almost right away when I found out that Poetry and I could hunt only until Dad and Mr. Thompson could get through here and meet us at Old Man Paddler's cabin. Then we would have to go on home and get our sleep.

"Growing boys need ten hours every night," Poetry's mother said, but it was just as bad as if my own mother had said it. It meant the same thing.

"As soon as we get through here," Dad said to Mr. Browne, "we'll take our wives home and drop Tom off at his house. And then, look out, Mr. Coon!" Dad's voice was filled with as much happiness as if he were only ten years old and ready to start for a circus.

Right that second I heard Tom Till's voice pipe up behind us, saying, "I'd better go now. Mother might be afraid to stay alone."

I jumped as if I had been shot, because his being there in the dark behind us meant he had probably heard everything Dad and Mr. Browne had said about his parents!

"Sure," Circus's father answered him, "we'll drive you home right now."

Little Jim found out what was going on, but his parents decided he couldn't go because he had on his best clothes, and it'd hold up the hunt if we had to wait for him to stop at his house and change.

So in a little while, Poetry and Tom Till and I drove away with Mr. Browne in his car. It must have seemed wonderful to our parents that they could let us go with him and not have to worry about us being in bad company, as they would have a year ago.

On the way we had to cross Wolf Creek bridge. We also had to *stop* there because there was a shock of corn standing right in the center of it!

"What on earth!" I said out loud.

Circus's dad answered, "Halloween."

"But Halloween's not till *tomorrow* night," I said, and so did Poetry.

But Little Tom Till, sitting beside Poetry in the backseat, didn't say a word. He did get out and help us get the shock of corn off the bridge and out into the side ditch, though, but all the time he kept on not saying a word.

"Boys will be boys," Circus's dad said. "I hope they don't do any serious damage to anybody's property."

I hoped so, too, but it didn't look as if I was going to be right. Several more times we had to stop to get the road unblocked, and whoever had done it had used somebody's farmyard gate or part of a fence to do it each time.

I was just boiling inside. I thought I knew who it was. The farther we drove, and the more pranks we ran into, the more I realized that Tom Till wasn't the only one who was caught in a trap. There was another red-haired, freckle-faced boy caught, too, in a different kind of a trap. Little Jim's mother's idea—that if the members of the Sugar Creek Gang were at the father-and-son banquet on Halloween night, we wouldn't get the blame for a lot of nonsensical things that some nonsensical vandals would do—well, it was a good idea. But she probably hadn't figured on what Big Bob Till and his gang would try to do to get even with our gang for having licked the stuffings out of them last summer in the Battle of Bumblebee Hill.

Bob and the rough-looking boys that had been with him at the produce house an hour or two ago were probably running wild all over the countryside tonight—the night *before* Halloween—taking gates off their hinges, setting up roadblocks, and who knew what else? And tomorrow our gang would get the blame for it!

But there was something even more worrisome than that on my mind, and it was Little Tom Till's being a thief. All the time as we drove along, getting farther and farther out into the country and nearer and nearer our house, I was thinking about what I had seen happen along the bayou that afternoon—and the four dollar bills that Tom Till had in his pocket right that minute as he sat behind me beside Poetry in the backseat.

In my mind's ear, also, I was hearing old Jay bawling on Little Tom's trail, getting closer and closer to him and finally treeing him, and—well, how *could* Tom do such a thing? How *could* he? He didn't seem that kind of boy at all.

Pretty soon we came to Dragonfly's house and crossed the little culvert at the foot of the last hill before you get to our place. There we ran into a fog bank so thick we had to slow to almost nothing so that we could see the road and not run off into the ditch.

At the top of the hill, the fog cleared a little, and in a little while we were stopping beside our mailbox. Poetry and I would go in, and I would change clothes.

Tom came tumbling out of the car after us, saying, "I'll get out here and walk the rest of the way."

He started to run, instead, down the road and toward the corner where it turns north and goes on toward the bridge. He only stayed on the road a few seconds, though. When he came to the place where the gang nearly always climbed over the fence to take the shortcut to the spring and the bridge, he made a dive for it, crawled through, and broke into a run to get home as fast as he could.

I knew that Tom knew the territory pretty well. He would not get lost even on a foggy night, which right that minute wasn't nearly as foggy as it had been. A second later I *knew* he could find his way.

"Hey!" I exclaimed to Poetry. "He's got a *flashlight!* I didn't know he *had* a flashlight!"

Poetry beside me giggled and said, "It's mine. I put the idea into his head so we could get started hunting quicker."

And that was another that. "You're almost bright," I answered.

"I'll get on home and get Circus and the dogs," Mr. Browne said, "and we'll be back right away. Circus'll be wondering what happened to me. I'm afraid the dogs will be getting impatient."

And away he went. It'd probably take him only ten or fifteen minutes, but we might not get to hunt long before we'd have to stop.

Poetry and I hurried across our moonlit lawn toward the house, and, being still thirsty, we stopped at the iron pitcher pump.

"Hey!" Poetry startled me with a yelp. "Some vandals have been here too!"

And sure enough, the handle of our pump was wired tightly to the rest of it with baling wire. The wire was wrapped round and round a dozen times. Well, that set my temper to boiling again, but there wasn't a thing I could do except to let it boil.

I got the kitchen-door key out of the secret place where we always kept it when we were away from home, and pretty soon Poetry and I were in the house. We didn't bother to take time to light any lamps but got Dad's long flashlight out of the cabinet drawer. Then we went upstairs to my room, where I had left my everyday clothes.

I had just stepped out of my Sunday pants and was about to step into my overalls when Poetry whispered excitedly, "I hear somebody outside!"

I quickly looked out the open window, not having remembered to shut it, as you are supposed to whenever you leave home—so that if it rains, you won't get your house all wet inside.

And Poetry was right. There was a noise like somebody doing something down by our barn near the load of high-nitrogen hay, which in the foggy moonlight was only a big rectangular shadow.

"Listen," Poetry whispered.

But I didn't even have to try to listen. The sound of the truck starting was loud enough to be heard twice as far away. I heard it not only with my ears but also with my conscience, because just that second the motor roared and the headlights went on, sending two long streams of foggy light across the barnyard and the tulip bed. And I began to remember an order Dad had given me in the afternoon, which was to get Mom's ring of keys out of the truck.

A sickening feeling scattered itself all over me and up and down my spine as I realized I was going to be partly to blame for somebody's stealing our truck. I had to do something *quick!*

It wasn't until I had galloped downstairs and was out by the tulip bed in the glaring headlights, yelling to the driver to stop and trying to flag him down with my overalls, that I realized I was wearing only a shirt and underwear—and, of course, my shoes and socks. And, for some reason, my cap.

I had seen pictures of boys waving handkerchiefs and shirts and things, trying to flag a train. I had read stories about that happening, and in the stories the trains always stopped. But this wasn't any train with a sensible engineer at the throttle. It was a truckload of baled hay with a driver who didn't seem to care what he ran into or over.

The driver started honking his horn at me, socking my ears with six or seven quick, sharp blasts followed by a fierce long one that was like a mad bull charging. The bright lights kept right on coming straight toward me, too, and I had to jump aside to keep from getting run over.

Then I accidentally stepped into the soft dirt of the tulip bed and fell down, and it looked as if it was going to be the end of a forgetful red-haired boy.

"Quick!" Poetry screamed. "Roll over! *Roll over!*"

And I did, twice, stopping only when I hit the pump platform, and I was safe.

The driver swerved right to miss the plum tree and went on toward the walnut tree and the open front gate.

Poetry's presence of mind was really good at a time like that. He'd gotten to the gate first, and he slammed it shut so that the driver couldn't get through. In a minute now, I thought, as I scrambled to my feet and started toward the center of things, there'd *really* be trouble, and it wouldn't be all mine.

Before I could get halfway there, though, the driver swung the truck to the left and steered it across the front yard—running over the rosebush under which Old Bushy-Tail had been digging that afternoon—then headed straight for the wooden gate that led to the orchard. That gate, thank goodness, was already shut, so we'd have the driver in a trap.

The only thing was, he wasn't slowing down but was going faster every second, as if he couldn't see the gate in the fog.

I was running after him, still waving my overalls and shouting. And Poetry was running along behind or beside me, hollering and waving Dad's flashlight. Both of us were yelling, *"Stop! Stop, thief!"*

And then, *whamety-swishety-crash!* That truck with Mom's keys in the ignition tore through our old wooden gate as if it had been made out of toothpicks, smashing it into maybe a hundred pieces of splintered lumber, and rumbled on out into the orchard.

If I hadn't been so mad and so scared and so worried and feeling so guilty for having forgotten to get Mom's keys, I might have laughed at what began to happen then. It was as funny as anything. The ropes Dad had used to tie on the bales of hay must have slipped loose. The first thing I knew, a bale had toppled off and onto the ground right between two big apple trees, two of the hungriest ones we had. And as the truck bounded on down through the orchard over the rough ground, every few dozen yards another bale of hay tumbled off.

But it wasn't any time to laugh—not for very long, anyway. In almost no time the truck came to the edge of the blackberry patch and started through it. It stopped a second later, unloading two more bales of hay at once because it had stopped so suddenly.

I knew what had happened. It had run into the old log that was in the center of the berry patch and on which, many a time, I had sat down to rest when I was picking berries and needing to eat a few for strength and so the pail wouldn't be too full to take to the house.

When the truck whammed into that log, it not only stopped, but the motor stopped, too. Maybe the driver thought his Halloween trick was finished and it was time to get out and run. Anyway he shoved open the door and leaped out.

Dad's powerful flashlight beam hit him full in the face at the same time. And I saw who it was—Big Bob Till himself. He had landed right in the middle of the thickest part of the blackberry patch, where the briars were the scratchiest.

I don't know how I happened to remember right that second the story of Brer Rabbit and the fox, but I did. Remember how the sly old fox thought he could punish the little bunny by throwing him into the bramble patch? Well, when I saw where Big Bob Till had landed, and thought how good it was for him to get a little punishment for all the Halloween tricks he had been playing that night, I started yelling what Brer Rabbit had yelled to Mr. Fox: "Born and bred in the bramble patch! Born and bred in the bramble patch!"

Poetry, hearing me, started yelling the same thing. For some reason I began to feel happy that Big Bob Till's epidermis was getting pierced by a lot of sharp, pointed instruments, so I kept on yelling, "Born and bred in the bramble patch! Born and bred in the *berry* patch!"

And that's where and when our fierce, fast fistfight started.

With two or three leaps, Bob Till was out of that blackberry patch and making straight for me. He got to me before I could have said "Jack Robinson Crusoe," and in a second both of his fists started landing all over me, as a lot of filthy words thundered into my ears.

"Try to make a Sunday school sissy out of my little brother, will you! Well, I'll show you, you little red-haired brat!"

For some reason, his calling me that helped me. I ignored his fast-flying fists, lowered my red head, and charged like a billy goat straight for his stomach, my own fists flying as fast as a windmill on a stormy day.

And then out of nowhere, it seemed, there came a sound of rushing feet, and a whole swarm of bigger boys were all over Poetry and me. One of them got Poetry down not more than ten feet from me and starting whamming him—*wham, wham, wham-wham—wham!*

Just as I told you when I started this story, I was angry enough to have licked my weight in wildcats. But, of course, you can't lick a wildcat with just a hot temper—or a great big bully, either, who for some reason seemed as big as the giant in the story of Jack and the Beanstalk. You have to fight with your fists and your feet and with every ounce of your eighty-seven pounds.

Maybe I could *almost* have licked Big Bob Till by himself, but he had all those other ruffians helping him, and in only a very few minutes I was getting the stuffings knocked out of me there in the foggy moonlight.

Then somebody's fist, which seemed even bigger than the one the giant had, landed on my chin, followed quick by what seemed a hundred others, and I knew I was licked. *Sock—wham—whoosh—double-sock—stars!* I actually *saw* stars, too. They were scattered all through my mind, and they seemed to be strung together with streaks of lightning.

Even while I was falling, I realized it wouldn't be good sense to fight anymore. I landed on a bale of high-nitrogen hay that happened to be there, then on the ground itself. Circus's dad had said it was a perfect night for coon. It would probably be a good night for possum too. Anyway, I did have sense enough to decide to do what I would have done naturally if I had been a North American marsupial—I would play possum. And I didn't have to pretend I was a dumb animal, when I was already a dumb *boy* for having left the keys in the truck in the first place.

Then I must have blacked out completely, because when I came to my senses, I thought I was hearing beautiful music. As soon as I knew enough to know what kind it was, I knew it was old Jay and Black and Tan whooping it up on a trail somewhere down along the bayou. Being still a little bit mixed up in my mind, it seemed I ought not to play possum any longer, or Black and Tan, who would trail North American marsupials as well as raccoons, might think I *was* one. Besides, who wanted to be sold to Tim Black at the produce house for only a little more than a muskrat was worth?

Bob and the other boys that had been in the fight were gone, and only Poetry and I and good old Circus were there. Circus quickly told me how, as soon as they could, he and his dad had come back with the car to get Poetry and me. Seeing the truck with its lights on in the blackberry patch, they stopped to find out why. And that had scattered the gang of rough boys, who beat it to their own car, parked in the ditch by the roadside, and they had driven away.

Poetry, who was sitting on a bale of high-nitrogen hay and holding his jaw, asked, "Where is the big lummox who socked me in the stomach?"

Well, we couldn't stay there in that foggy moonlight talking about a lost fight, when Blue Jay and Black and Tan were whooping it up on a hot trail down along the bayou, so I got to my feet to see if I was all right. I was, except that I had to look around to find my overalls, which had been such a failure as a flag for stopping the truck.

When I had them on, I said to Poetry, "Let me have the flashlight, will you?" A little later I was working my way through a lot of sharp-pointed instruments, being especially careful of my epidermis, to Dad's truck. Shining the light inside, I saw Mom's key ring hanging there with the key still in the ignition switch.

Boy oh boy, you can guess I put those keys into one of my overalls pockets as quick as I could, sighing a big sigh of relief at the same time.

Then, feeling finer than I really should have, I was in the mood for another adventure. Circus's dad and the hounds were already on the way, and in a jiffy Poetry and Circus and I would be down along the bayou where they were.

The only thing was, I still had to go back to the house to get my everyday jacket, as the dampness of the night would make Mom make me put it on if she were there.

Also, I didn't have my boots, and it would be wet and sloppy in some places. It didn't feel good to have to waste so much time, but I knew I'd have to have the jacket and boots. So away we ran through the orchard and through the splintered gate to my house.

There, I realized that I'd have to leave a note for my folks, or they'd see the truck was gone and also see the broken gate, and Dad might even see the truck itself out in the blackberry patch, and Mom would be worried sick.

"Don't worry about anything funny you see

around the place," my note stated. "I didn't get hurt a bit, and everything is fine. I changed my clothes like you told me to, and I've got my boots on, and my jacket—which I don't need, because I'm plenty warm yet. If you're thirsty, just take the wire off the pump. I didn't have time to do it myself."

Hurry—hurry—hurry, my mind kept saying to me as Poetry held the flashlight while I wrote and old Jay and Black and Tan kept on whooping it up down along the bayou, having the time of their lives.

It seemed almost an hour, although it couldn't have been more than a few minutes, before I had the note finished and we could be on our way. Those minutes had gone even slower than when I had stood on the chair in the afternoon!

"Come on!" I exclaimed to Circus and Poetry as we started on the gallop toward our mailbox.

In a little while we came to the spring, where the dogs were, and they were having trail trouble. Their noses told them a coon had been there somewhere, but it was as if he had been a ghost coon. The smell of his tracks had evaporated, and all they could do was run around in worried circles up and down the creek and around the Black Widow Stump, where Circus's dad had almost lost his life. Then they ran along the rail fence, where in the afternoon Poetry and Dragonfly and I had seen Little Tom Till steal the muskrat out of the trap.

For a while it looked as if the hounds had lost the scent for good, but a little later, after maybe fifteen minutes, old Jay struck it again about halfway between the spring and the bridge, and the chase was really on.

Over the fence, across the north road, and over the fence on the other side we went as fast as those dogs' noses could take us. In about seven minutes we came to the place where I had taken the flip-flop into the colony of Canada thistle. This time I managed to dodge them.

As we swished past, Poetry puffed out part of the poem again, saying, "And away they all flew like the down of a thistle."

The farther we went, the more I realized we were following the same trail we had followed that afternoon. Circus and I were side by side for a minute, and I said to him, "I wonder if they're following Little Tom Till's boot tracks again."

When I said that, he almost shouted at me, "Why do you have to believe the *worst* about one of my best friends?"

I guess I hadn't realized just how much he really liked that little red-haired guy.

Then we both stopped. Right that minute the dogs were having trouble again, whining and whimpering around an old rail fence, trying to decide how come they couldn't smell which side the coon had gone on.

I decided then would be a good time for

me to nose out the Little Tom Till trail I was on myself, by telling Circus what had happened at the produce house in town that night— although maybe, I thought, his father had already told him part of it.

It took me only a few minutes to give Circus the whole story. I finished by saying, "And Little Tom Till picked up that money and put it in his pocket!"

"I don't believe it," Circus answered me, leaping over a log only a second before I did.

The two of us sat down on it to rest awhile.

"But I saw it with my own eyes!" I answered. "I actually *saw* those muskrats come tumbling out of that gunnysack, and I saw Mr. Black pay Tom Till a dollar apiece for them!"

"You forget that Tom didn't carry that gunnysack into the produce house the *first* time. His father did. You told me that yourself."

"But I *saw* Tom Till steal one this afternoon right on the other side of the bayou! If he could steal *one*, he could steal *four!*"

"I still don't believe it," Circus answered stubbornly. "Old Jay wouldn't be dumb enough to trail a pair of wet shoes, because there wouldn't be enough coon scent on them to fool him."

"How do you know that?" I asked. "He trailed Tom until he had to take to a tree to keep from getting caught on the ground, didn't he?"

"Dad says no. Not the way they make coon-skin caps nowadays. They treat them with chemicals and stuff, and there wouldn't be any coon scent on them like there would be in Daniel Boone's days, when they made them out of raw furs."

"But I *saw* Tom Till take a muskrat out of your trap," I insisted.

Circus answered with something that helped me to realize what a nice person he himself was: "Tom wouldn't do a thing like that to me. He's my little brother."

Just then old Black and Tan, about a hundred yards ahead of us in the direction of the swamp, let out a long, quavering bawl, which meant he had hit the trail again and it was really hot.

Away we went after him.

Even as we galloped on, I was thinking how much Circus really liked that little guy, and for some reason I got a warm feeling inside of me. It seemed kind of wonderful that anybody could like anybody else that well, and for a minute it seemed it wouldn't be right for me to say or do anything to keep Circus from loving Little Tom Till, whom he was making believe was his little brother. I also was remembering something Dad had planted like a seed in my mind one day: "Everybody *has* to love something or somebody. God made people that way."

Right then, to my surprise and also to my worry, I heard both hounds bark "treed." First Blue Jay's trembling, high-pitched wail changed to a short, deeper-voiced, excited bark that seemed to say, "Hey, you slow-running, only two-legged human beings! I've got him treed! Hurry up and come and get him!" Then old Black and Tan joined in with his own changed voice, saying the same thing, and my mind was interested in the chase again, wondering what would happen next.

It took only a little while to reach the swamp. And there, to my absolute astonishment, everything was almost exactly as it had been in the afternoon. The only difference was that this time there were *two* hounds instead of one, making twice as much excited noise and barking up the same linden tree Tom had been up.

Circus's dad was shooting his strong spotlight up through the foggy air into the branches of the leafless tree, and I shot my eyes up to where the light was focused, to see what I could see. That little saucer-shaped light darted from the trunk out along every gray branch, zigzagging back and forth until the whole tree had been searched. And there not only wasn't any nice gray brown, black-checked, ring-tailed coon up there anywhere, but there was nothing at all.

9

The coon must have come down the tree almost as quick as it had gone up—if it actually had gone up in the first place, which I doubted.

"What did I tell you?" I whispered to Circus when we had all decided there wasn't any coon up there. "The dogs followed his boot tracks to the tree again."

Circus didn't even answer me. Instead he said to the hounds, "Listen, you! You're barking up the wrong tree! Let's get going!" Then he let out a long, high-pitched hunter's call, which, as that kind of call always does, sent an excited chill zigzagging around in my mind and all over me.

Mr. Browne let out the same kind of call, and the dogs looked up at both their masters with questions in their eyes. Then, when we all started on deeper into the swamp, they left the linden tree and ran ahead of us down the creek.

We hadn't gone more than a hundred yards when, just as he had done in the afternoon, old Jay came to excited hound life with another bawl, saying in hound language, "I've found it, and it's one of the biggest coons that ever lived along Sugar Creek!" A second later, Black and Tan's voice was bawling the same thing.

Away we all went again, bounding through the swamp as fast as we could.

"Hey!" Poetry exclaimed from beside or behind me somewhere. "He's headed for the hills again, toward Old Man Paddler's cabin!"

"Sure," I answered. "He's a smart coon. He knows where half of our parents are supposed to meet us."

Zip-zip-zip, crunch-crunch-crunch, swish-swish-swish, over logs and around chokecherry shrubs and papaw bushes and brush piles and colonies of Canada thistle, and on and on and on we ran. We were getting onto higher ground all the time and still going in the direction of Old Man Paddler's clapboard-roofed cabin.

The living daylights that had been knocked out of me beside the bale of high-nitrogen hay had come back in again, and I was feeling wonderful. I had been born and bred in a bramble patch, and getting knocked out in a fight was something I was getting used to. After a while, when we had caught the coon, we would see Old Man Paddler, and would I ever have a fine story to tell Dad when I saw *him!* It would be hard to tell him about the fight, though, without mentioning the truck being in the orchard.

"In the orchard!" he would say. "How did it get *there?* I left it in the barnyard!"

That was as far ahead as I got to think right then, because things began to happen fast up ahead of us. Most of the fog was gone here in the hills. I could see quite a ways in every direction. And right that minute I saw something run across a little strip of moonlight and disappear in the shadow of the evergreens that bordered the path leading from Old Man Paddler's spring to his cabin. It went so fast I couldn't have decided what it was even if I had been a lot closer, but it looked the height of an extra-large timber wolf. The only thing was, it seemed to be running on its hind legs.

At almost the same time, both hounds' voices changed again, sounding as though somebody had thrown a blanket over them and they were being smothered.

"They've caught him on the *ground!*" Circus cried. "Let's get there quick, or they'll tear his fur to shreds!"

We *really* ran then, getting to where the hounds were in only a few seconds, all of us scolding the dogs at the same time and ordering them to stop. We knew they'd puncture that coon's skin with their big sharp teeth, and it wouldn't be worth more than half as much at the produce house. Also, those hounds might get their own ears slit. Coons can do that to a dog's ears in a flash of a second in a face-to-face fight, and sometimes a hound gets the living daylights scratched out of him.

"Why, look!" Circus cried. "He's caught in a trap."

And that's exactly what his dad's flashlight showed us was the truth. That middle-sized, furry ringtail had its left hind leg caught in the jaws of a savage-looking, double-springed steel trap.

I noticed that the ring on the other end of the trap's steel coil chain was fastened to a forked stick.

In seconds, Circus and his dad had both old Jay and his dog pal Black and Tan by their collars and were holding them back from whatever they wanted to do to the coon.

Poetry exclaimed then, "They've already killed it! It's already dead!"

And it wasn't any huge, fierce-fighting coon at all, I thought, if it could get licked as easily as that. Actually, it wasn't much bigger than a big fat possum and maybe wouldn't weigh more than ten pounds. And it wasn't moving a muscle.

"That's the trap I had set down by the spring!" Circus said. "For muskrats."

"No wonder he couldn't climb very high up the linden tree," I thought to say, "with that big steel trap fastened to him."

"Yeah, no wonder," Poetry answered. "Poor little guy. He must have had a hard time dragging that trap all the way through the swamp. He's all covered with mud."

Neither Circus nor his dad said anything. They were studying the coon, maybe looking it over for size and teeth marks, hoping its fur wasn't badly damaged by the hounds' teeth.

Pretty soon, after both dogs had been petted and praised a little for doing such nice nose work, and after they had acted pleased half to death by being liked so well, we had the coon out of the trap and were on our way to Old Man Paddler's cabin. It was just ahead of us farther up the hill, and we were supposed to meet Dad and Poetry's dad there as soon as they could come from helping in the church basement.

In only a little while we came to within sight of the light in the old man's window. Even though I'd been there dozens of times, there was always something about going up to see that kind old man that made me feel fine. Also, there was always something about a light in a country window at night that made me feel fine, especially in the Collins family's kitchen window when Dad and I were on our way home from somewhere and it was suppertime.

The light in Old Man Paddler's kitchen window meant he was still up and maybe even waiting for us, having heard the hounds and seen our lights. Or else he might be reading or writing letters. Anyway, we knew that as soon as we got there he'd want us to drink a cup of sassafras tea with him.

Another reason I was feeling fine inside was that I knew—even though the coon was only a middle-sized one—that its fur would bring twice as much as a muskrat's. Circus could have it skinned and could sell it tomorrow and have at least two dollars to give to the Alaska missionary offering tomorrow night.

Thinking that, though, started me to thinking about Tom Till again, and it was just like a giant had blown out the lamplight in my mind.

As we trudged along, Mr. Browne, carrying the muddy coon, was quite a ways ahead of

Poetry and me. Circus, carrying the empty trap, was quite a ways behind us. Poetry wasn't satisfied about something or other, and he said so when we came to the evergreen border and the path that led to the old man's spring. "There's something fishy about a coon dragging a trap like that clear through the swamp and getting mud all over itself like that. Coons are as careful as a house cat about keeping their fur clean."

"That swamp's pretty muddy in places," I said.

He answered, "Yes, but coons don't stand on their heads or roll around on their backs in the mud."

"Hear that?" I whispered, all of a sudden having heard a voice behind us somewhere.

We both listened, and it was somebody singing. *Singing!*

"It's Circus," Poetry said. "Listen a minute."

The voice was coming from away back at the farther end of the row of evergreens, but the words were almost as clear as if they were coming from a tape deck:

"There's a light in the window of heaven—
  It is shining for someone tonight;
  And the Father is watching beside it—
  He's keeping it shining and bright."

Of course, I'd know Circus's voice anywhere. He had one of the best boy-soprano voices in the whole territory. And to hear it echoing out across the Sugar Creek hills at night—well, it sent a little glad feeling all through me.

"I'll bet he's going to sing tomorrow night," Poetry decided, "and he's practicing."

I already knew that was the truth.

It certainly was a pretty song. I couldn't get all the words, but hearing it while we were close enough to Old Man Paddler's cabin to see the light in his window made me think about God for a minute. And my mind's eye was seeing Him waiting up in heaven beside *His* window, looking for someone to come home and keeping the light burning for anybody who didn't know the way. Without knowing I was going to do it—and forgetting for a second or two that Poetry was there with me—I heard my own voice saying to Somebody I liked better than anyone else, "I hope Little Tom Till gets saved soon. He's a pretty neat little guy. But maybe You already know that."

Poetry, not knowing who I was talking to, said, "Yeah, I know it. But how come he dragged that coon all the way up here? Why didn't he take it on home with him?"

"How come *what*?" I asked, absolutely astonished.

"You don't *really* think a coon would stand on its head and roll over on its back in a muddy swamp, do you? No sir, that coon was dragged up here by somebody. He found it in the trap down by the spring, killed it, and half carried and half dragged it all the way to where the hounds almost caught up with him. It was too heavy for a boy Tom's size to carry all that way, so it kept touching the ground every so often. And that's how the hounds managed to trail it. When they almost caught up with him, he left it and beat it out into the woods somewhere."

And then is when I remembered the shadow I had seen of something as big as a timber wolf, running on its hind legs across a strip of moonlight toward the same evergreens we were in right that very second.

What Poetry had said made sense, but for some reason I didn't want it to. Of course, if Tom would steal a muskrat, he could do the same thing to a coon. "But he went on home after he left our house," I objected. "We saw him go ourselves."

"We saw him *start* home," Poetry said. "But he was headed down the path to the spring on the shortcut to the bridge when we *last* saw him."

"I don't want to believe it," I countered, and I didn't.

While we were all in the old man's cabin, waiting for two of our fathers to get through at the church and come to where we were, Circus's dad decided it would be a good idea to skin the coon. Then they could carry it along with them on the rest of the hunt, and whoever had to carry it wouldn't get too tired.

"That's certainly a fine fur," Old Man Paddler said. "It looks like a brother to one I caught myself night before last out back of the woodpile."

He chuckled a little and added, "Can't quite get over being a boy. My twin brother, Kenneth, and I used to trap this whole territory."

Pretty soon Theodore Collins and Leslie Thompson's father came driving up the lane. And because Dad's long, shaggy eyebrows were too low for my comfort, I right away was in the middle of telling him what had happened at the house and in the orchard with the bales of high-nitrogen hay. To my relief, Dad—being the kind of father who sometimes forgets his keys himself—didn't have even one discouraging word to say about the whole thing. "I'm just glad you are alive. You are, aren't you?" he asked.

Poetry answered for me by pinching me till I said, "Ouch!" to prove I was not only alive but still able to fight a little.

"You have your mother's keys now?" Dad asked. As I handed them over, he said, "Thank you, my son. You're a very thoughtful boy. You found them in the orchard, I believe."

My heart was as light as a feather as we talked. It was wonderful not to get scolded for something I had already made up my mind I would never do again if I could help it. "I found them in the bramble patch where I was born and bred," I answered.

He put his arm around me partway—as he does when he likes me and thinks it won't hurt me to know it—and he said in a friendly, sarcastic voice, "You must have changed your pants down there somewhere."

"The funny thing about it is, I *did,*" I said, not having told him that part of the story yet.

Poetry cut in with: "The 'funny thing,' is right." And he launched into a fast-talking story of how ridiculous I looked changing my clothes in the shade of the old apple tree beside a bale of high-nitrogen hay.

"We'll get going on those trees in the morning," Dad said, "after you've had a good night's sleep. Poor trees. They'll be pretty hungry, having their breakfast right beside them all night and not being able to eat even one little rootful."

"You're a fun father," I said. "I'd rather have you for a father than any father I ever had." I was *really* feeling fine. Maybe he would even let me go on hunting with the rest of them.

The "rest of them" were out by Old Man Paddler's woodshed at the time, and only Poetry had listened in on our father-and-son visit.

But Dad quickly proved he was another kind of father, too, not being able to change his mind on something he thought was important. And since Poetry's father was not able to change his either, pretty soon their two boys were getting ready to start in a hurry toward home.

"So your mother won't worry," Dad said, "if she asks about her keys, tell her I have them."

Circus, in spite of being worried about the

furs being taken from his traps and knowing why Poetry and I really had to go home—which was because we were growing boys and needed a lot more sleep than grown-up persons do—said, "I'm pretty young myself. I'll go along with you," which Mr. Browne agreed to.

The three of us soon started down the little path between the evergreens to the old man's private spring. As soon as we were alone, Circus said, "On the way I'm going to take a look at the traps along the bayou. Want to go along?"

And that's how come we found out that foggy moonlit night exactly who had been taking fur from his traps. And did we *ever* find out. And were we ever surprised! I mean *surprised!*

10

It had been a wonderful night as well as a wonderful afternoon. Both of them had been packed with enough excitement to satisfy any ordinary boy, but for some reason I was still like old Jay on a lost coon trail. I was on the trail of a trapline thief, and I wouldn't be satisfied till I treed him.

Just as the three of us started following our own noses down the path between the evergreens, I heard Mr. Browne's voice giving the hunter's call from somewhere on the other side of the cabin. For a second I turned and looked back up the hill to watch. The three men with the two hounds were starting off in the direction of the old man's apple orchard, where they hoped the dogs would get into a face-to-face fight with a North American marsupial that had been helping herself to some of the neighbors' chickens and which would probably decide to get licked as soon as the dogs started the fight—as you are supposed to do when you get into a fight in an apple orchard.

We stopped at the old man's spring for a drink, then started on, walking in the small circle of light made by Dad's flashlight, which we still had. We hadn't gone more than fifty feet in the direction of the sycamore tree when we heard running steps behind us.

A second later something shot out of the shadows into the moonlight, heading straight toward us like a big timber wolf running on its hind legs.

When you've already had one fight and gotten licked, and your chin hurts, and you're kind of tired, anyway, and have had your epidermis pricked with pins and Canada thistles, and have been in a whirlwind of excitement all day and all night so far, and something—you can't tell what—is running toward you across a stretch of foggy moonlight like a timber wolf on its hind legs—well, you really wonder what will happen next.

And then, what to my wondering eyes should appear but a boy in a coonskin cap carrying an air rifle and a gunnysack, and it was Little Tom Till himself. "Quick!" he panted. "Somebody's going to follow your trapline tonight, Circus, and take all your muskrats. We've got to stop him."

Tom was so excited and out of breath from running that he couldn't talk straight. But he made enough sense for us to understand he had found out someway that somebody was going to follow Circus's trapline and steal everything that was already caught, and maybe he was already doing it.

It didn't make sense, though, for *Tom* to be telling us, when that very afternoon I had seen him take a muskrat himself. Probably right that very minute he had four dollars in one of his pockets, which I had seen Mr. Black give him for four muskrats not more than three hours ago.

Away we all went, though, as fast as we could. We didn't stop to figure out how four kind of smallish boys could capture a thief if we suddenly came upon him while he was taking anything out of a trap—or how we could manage to hold him if he turned out to be two or three giant-sized boys as big as the ones that had swarmed all over us in our orchard.

Just as we ran past the sycamore tree and headed in the direction of the colony of Canada thistle, Circus asked Tom, "How do you *know* somebody's going to do it?"

Tom was running ahead of the rest of us at the time. "Can't you run any faster?" he answered from over his shoulder. "Come on, everybody!" And that little guy started to run even faster as he led the way for us back toward the Sugar Creek bridge and the bayou, where Circus had most of his traps.

At the spring, Circus looked at the place where he had had his double-springed trap set for a muskrat and had caught a ten-pound coon instead. We stopped just long enough to decide we would go to the place where somebody had taken a muskrat out of a trap that afternoon, and there we would hide in the thicket and wait.

"Who do you think it'll be?" I asked as we crossed the little rivulet and went on up the other side of the bayou. I was wishing Big Jim was with us. He could really lick his weight in wildcats. *Why hadn't we thought to go and get him before we started on such a dangerous adventure?* I wondered.

While we were waiting there in the dark in that thick thicket, it seemed the whole Indian summer night was alive with sounds. If it hadn't been such a tense time, with wondering what on earth was going to happen, I think I would have enjoyed sitting there.

There were still a few crickets that hadn't quit chirping. Two or three of them were right close to the log we were sitting on. For a second I let my mind's eye watch one of those cute little black insects as he vibrated his forewings together, sounding like a baby chicken just learning to peep and being afraid to.

Every now and then, from somewhere up the bayou, a night heron let out a spooky, *"Quoke-quoke,"* which sounded as if he had had too many frogs and minnows for supper and was trying to swallow backward.

Right in the middle of my listening and thinking, a boy's elbow pressed into my side, and Poetry hissed, "*Sh!* Somebody's coming! From the direction of the spring!"

I looked as best I could through the tall weeds and saw a flashlight go on and off as fast as a firefly's fleeting flash. A second later I heard somebody coming along the path we ourselves had been on fifteen minutes ago. In only a few seconds we would know who it was.

We had agreed that, as soon as anybody came, we would flash our lights into his face, and all of us would see him at the same time.

Every few seconds we saw the flashlight go on and off as he came nearer and nearer. We didn't dare move, or we might be heard ourselves, and we hardly dared breathe.

We certainly *were* breathing though, sounding like four boys that had been running in a fast race and had stopped to rest. I could even hear my heart beating, so loud it almost drowned out every other sound.

Then Circus whispered, "Somebody's coming from *up* the creek too!"

And sure enough, somebody was. He was almost as close as the person who was coming from the direction of the spring.

It looked as if they might both get there at the same time, but they didn't. The one from down the creek got there first. He stopped at the very same place where in the afternoon Tom Till or somebody else had gone down the little incline to the water's edge and helped himself to the muskrat.

He flashed on his light, shot its beam all around, into the water, and out at the muskrat houses. At the same time I could hear that other person coming from the other direction. I could hear the sound of corn blades rustling as he worked his way through Dragonfly's dad's cornfield.

Just then the flashlight near the water accidentally lit up the person's face, and I saw who it was. I gasped aloud and couldn't help it. He jumped as though he'd been scared half to death, just as the boy this afternoon had when Dragonfly sneezed.

But it wasn't my fault. Anybody who is a member of the Sugar Creek Gang would have done the same thing. Circus himself couldn't keep still, and he exclaimed under his breath, "It's *Big Jim!*"

And then things really began to happen. Like a shot, somebody else came dashing out from the shadows along the shore. And at almost the same time, a half-dozen other boys exploded from all around us like a covey of quail and flew like two-legged arrows for Big Jim, all of them getting there at about the same time.

Before Big Jim could straighten up, those big rough boys—or men, whichever they were—scooped him up, lifted him struggling and kicking and squirming, and hurled him out into the water, where he landed with a moonlit splash about seven feet from shore at the edge of a muskrat igloo.

And that woke up all the rest of the night creatures that were along the bayou, I being one of them. I knew, without even having to think, that somebody had played a mean trick on Big Jim. I shot like a red-haired, two-legged charging bull straight for that huddle of rough-looking boys—knowing who they probably were—and struck like a bale of high-nitrogen hay right in the center of all of them.

I think I expected to bowl them over and send them hurtling out into the water where Big Jim had landed, but for five reasons I didn't. Those five ruffians were the five reasons. I not only didn't do what I wanted to, but I *did* do what I didn't want to.

Instead of ramming those guys in the stomach as I'd planned, I ran into their hands, which were waiting for me the way I wait for Charlotte Ann when she comes running toward me. Two or three pairs of strong arms caught me up like a cottontail rabbit and whirled me through the air, swinging me back and forth twice. Then away I went with the greatest of ease out through the foggy moonlight in the direction of an igloo-shaped muskrat house. A second later I landed with a noisy splash in the cold bayou water.

Almost before you could say "Jack Robinson Crusoe," if you had wanted to, two other boys were in the water beside Big Jim and me. They were barrel-shaped Poetry and Circus, our acrobat. Where Tom Till was, I didn't know and didn't find out till later.

But no sooner than we had landed in the water and started splashing around to get to our feet, there was a loud chorus of guffaws from the shore. That bunch of roughnecks who had worked such a mean trick on us started yelling with coarse, throaty voices and spilling a lot of filthy words from their dirty minds at the same time.

"Born and bred in the muskrat pond! Born

and bred in the muskrat pond! *Born and bred in the muskrat pond!*"

One of the boys' voices was Big Bob Till's.

Then there was the noise of running feet as that whole gang rushed up the slope into Dragonfly's dad's cornfield and disappeared.

Even before we could get to shore, Poetry's nearly always cheerful mind was working to make what had happened to us seem less humiliating. He said, "Well, that's *one* Halloween trick the Sugar Creek Gang won't get the blame for tomorrow night."

But Circus was thinking something sober. "Where's Tom?" he asked.

We could still hear the sound of running feet, going now in the direction of the old swimming hole.

And Big Jim had thoughts of his own. He came storming out of that water with his temper boiling. "Come on!" he ordered us. "Let's get 'em!"

And away went four sopping-wet, mad-as-hornets boys through Dragonfly's dad's cornfield in the direction the other boys had gone. *Squish, splashety, swish.*

But it was like looking for a bunch of needles in a haystack to find those guys in the fog, which seemed to be getting thicker again.

At the creek we stopped, thinking we heard something on the other side. Then Big Jim let out another half-dozen angry words, saying, "The dirty crooks! They've cut our boat loose! It's gone!"

And from across the creek we heard some-body laugh a loud, coarse laugh and say, "It's over on *this* side, if you want it. Good night, you guys! Hope you sleep well. Sorry we couldn't wait till tomorrow night to give you your Satur-day night bath!"

And that was that. We stood there boiling inside and grinding our teeth, but there wasn't any use to waste good temper on something we couldn't do anything about. We'd better go home and change our clothes and get some sleep.

Just then I heard, coming from the direc-tion of Old Man Paddler's cabin away up in the hills, the long, high-pitched bawl of old Blue Jay, who seemed to be running happily along on a hot coon trail.

"Where is Tom Till?" Circus asked us all again.

My mind asked the same question.

Where *was* he?

11

Tom Till had disappeared like Little Bo Peep's sheep, and we didn't know where to find him. We could, of course, leave him alone, and he would go home with the tail of his coonskin cap bobbing behind him.

I was still as lost in my mind as a hound who has lost the trail of a coon. Tom had disappeared while the rest of us were splashing our way out of the muskrat pond where we had been born and bred. He had disappeared while his big brother, Bob, and his tough town gang were scattering their way through the cornfield, getting into the Sugar Creek Gang's rowboat, which we kept chained to a willow at the swimming hole, and rowing across.

Big Jim was interested in where Tom had gone, too, but for a different reason. As we stood in our dripping clothes there on the bank, after the coarse laughter from the other side of the creek had stabbed us in the heart, he said to Circus, "It was a dirty trick. The little rascal lied to me. He called me on the phone an hour ago and told me there was a coon in one of your traps down along the bayou and he knew for sure somebody was going to follow your line for a Halloween trick and steal everything. He wanted me to come and get it. Said you had gone hunting and didn't know about it."

"An *hour* ago?" Poetry said. "How come you just got here, then?"

"I told him it wasn't any of my business and, besides, Halloween wasn't till tomorrow night. And I hung up. Then, after I heard your hounds up in the hills, I got to thinking maybe I *ought* to go down and look. So I did, and— what a dirty trick! I never thought Little Tom would do it. I suppose a brother will do anything for a brother, though. But let me get my hands on just *one* of them!"

And right then is when we heard Little Tom Till's voice calling us from somewhere down along the bayou, saying, "Hey, Bill! Circus! Poetry! Come and help me!"

We started on the run in the direction his voice had come from, and in a few minutes we were by the willow against which he had leaned his air rifle that afternoon.

The little guy was down at the water's edge, with his small flashlight in one hand, holding for dear life onto a forked stick that had a trap chain fastened to it. On the other end of the chain, caught in the trap, was a muskrat. And on the other end of the muskrat, thrashing about in the water and holding onto the muskrat for dear life was a huge snapping turtle, the biggest one I had ever seen.

Even before we could get to Tom to help him, there was a violent splashing and boiling of the water, and it was too late to save the muskrat.

"He's *got* it!" Tom cried. "He's stole one of Circus's muskrats!"

And now, *What on earth? What on earth!* I thought. Right in front of my surprised and astonished eyes I had seen the Sugar Creek trapline thief, and he was a big, vicious-headed snapping turtle!

Circus surprised me by saying, "There, you smart guys! *That's* what's been stealing my fur! *That's* why I find all my traps down here thrown and nothing in them! The snapping turtles have been getting 'em!"

I knew something was wrong with that idea, though, and so did Big Jim and Poetry. Big Jim spoke up in a skeptical voice, saying to Tom, "What about the coon you told me was in the trap down here somewhere? Was that just your imagination?"

"I saw him when I was on my way home. That's why I phoned you. There *was* a coon, but when you said it wasn't any of your business, and I knew Bob—I mean, I knew somebody was going to follow the line and take everything, I came back myself. I started to take him to Old Man Paddler's. I knew he'd fix everything up for me."

Tom started talking like a house afire then, and it seemed he was trying to talk himself out of being a thief, as much as I didn't like to believe he was.

Four of us were standing there as wet as drowned muskrats while Tom, with the empty trap chain in his hand and as dry as a corn blade on a sunshiny day, kept trying to explain everything.

I cut in on him once, asking, "How about the muskrat I saw you take out of the trap this afternoon—and the four you sold to Mr. Black tonight? I suppose the snapping turtle took them too, and you got them away from him!"

"No sir, I took 'em myself. I found out somebody was going to run the traps tonight, so I put on my daddy's old hunter's coat and got them myself. I already had three before you saw me."

"And old Jay trailed you up a tree," Poetry said. "See there, Bill Collins? What did I tell you?"

"But you sold those four muskrats and kept the money," I accused Tom, feeling mad at him as well as at his brother. *Somebody* ought to be blamed for my being all wet!

"I took them home and put them in a gunnysack and hid them in the barn. I was going to give them to Circus as soon as I had a chance or maybe take them up to Old Man Paddler's to get him to help me. I had five pigeons in another gunnysack I was going to sell so I could have something to give tomorrow night, and—" and then Tom's voice broke "all—all the rest of my pigeons got out and flew away while I was trying to get the five I wanted."

I could see then that Tom felt worse about having lost his pigeons than about anything else. He didn't seem to have any idea that he had done wrong in taking the muskrats, which it looked as if he was trying to lie his way out of.

Over on the other side of the pond there was another splashing and a *"Quoke-quoke,"* as though the heron was *really* losing his supper, or maybe he had been listening to Tom's mixed-up story himself and couldn't stomach it.

But Tom was almost finished. His trembling, tearful voice hurried on. "Bob found out I was going to sell the pigeons, and he told me I couldn't. He said half of them were his and that I had let my half fly away. And he took the sack and—and I guess he sold them to Mr. Black tonight."

"And *you* sold the four muskrats!" I said. For a minute it seemed I was a detective questioning somebody we had arrested on suspicion.

"Daddy knew I wanted to sell my pigeons too. He was half drunk all day, and when he found the gunnysack in the barn, he thought it was them. Here. Here's the four dollars!" he said to Circus. "I'm sorry I caused so much trouble—"

Then the little guy's voice broke into a thousand tears, and he couldn't finish. He only said, "And here, take your old trap!" He swung around and broke into a fast run down the path toward the spring.

Like a shot, Circus was after him, and the rest of us were after Circus, who caught Tom after he had run just a short way.

But that little guy struggled and fought like a trapped tiger, saying, "You won't believe me! You think I'm a thief! You hate my daddy!"

Circus held onto him, pinning his arms to his sides so that he couldn't hurt anybody with his fast-flying fists. "I do too believe you. I believed you all the time. You did it for *me*. You were trying to save my furs."

"I wasn't *either*," Tom blurted out. "I was trying to keep Bob from having to go to jail again! I took them so that he *couldn't* take them. Let me loose." And he began to fight again.

In the struggle, his cap brushed against my face, and what to my wondering nose should appear but a smell that was almost exactly like the fur of a coon that had just been skinned. Because I was still doubting him a little, I asked, "And where did you get this cap? Where did you get the money to pay for it?"

"Old Man Paddler *gave* it to me yesterday. He *made* it. He used to help his mother make coonskin caps when he was a little boy. He wanted me to have one like he and his twin brother used to wear."

"Let me *smell* it," Circus said in a kind voice.

I was remembering what the old man had said a little over a half hour ago about having caught a coon himself night before last out behind his woodpile.

While Circus was smelling the coonskin cap, Poetry and I were smelling Tom's hair, and *it* smelled like coonskin, too.

"What did I tell you?" Poetry exclaimed. "No wonder those dogs trailed him."

And then it seemed everything was clear in my mind, and I began to feel fine. "You're a great little guy," I said to Tom. "You're one of my best friends."

"And we believe everything you've told us," Big Jim said. "I'm sorry I said what I said back there."

And then, just as it had happened before when I was at the grape arbor and Tom had handed my mother a drink of water, it was as if somebody had gone to the blackboard on which all Little Tom Till's sins were written and erased every one of them. I guess it was just in my own mind that all those mean things had been written, anyway.

"I've got to get home quick and get into bed before Bob gets there and wonders where I am," Tom said.

In spite of the weather's being warm, for some reason Poetry and Circus and Big Jim and I were almost shivering. But we went with Tom Till all the way to the Sugar Creek bridge, anyway, and there we left him.

"I'll see you tomorrow," I said to Tom. "You and I are going to help my dad feed the apple trees in the morning."

"OK!" Tom called. And away he ran, his feet making a friendly noise as he scurried across the bridge toward his house.

As the rest of us walked up the road toward where it would turn to go toward my house, I thought I heard a different kind of noise, one I hadn't heard for a whole year. "Listen to that," I said, stopping in the gravel road.

Poetry and Big Jim and Circus also stopped to listen.

I listened toward the sky, where the sound was coming from. The noise was some of the sweetest music we ever hear around Sugar Creek in the fall. It was the honking of Canada geese going South for the winter. I knew if it had been daytime and I could have seen them, I'd have seen fifteen or twenty flying in formation, making a wide V-shaped trail through the sky. If I had been one of them, flying along, we all would have looked just alike, having dark bodies and black heads and pretty white patches under our chins.

It would be kind of wonderful, wouldn't it —being a Canada goose, flying with long, slow, measured wing beats through the moonlit sky on the way to a warm summer climate?